Preface

CASTLE OF DREAMS and the Blue Butterfly is the second book in a series of fictional fantasy tales for early and young readers. The concept for the book series came about after completing the first book, *Castle of Dreams and the Dragon Princess.* That book was written to tell the story behind my acoustic solo piano CD, *Castle of Dreams Acoustic Solo Piano.* The CD consists of sixteen piano compositions, which will one day be a ballet.

The story takes place in the middle ages. A time when castles were prominent and kingdoms were ruled by royal families. Megan, the main character, is the daughter of the queen's head chambermaid. She grows up in the castle along with the prince. The book series, "Castle of Dreams" tells

the tale of their adventures in the magical and
mystical time of castles, kings, queens, knights,
sorcerers and dragons.

CASTLE OF DREAMS
and the
Blue Butterfly

David Michael Walsh & Janet Walsh

Published in the USA by:
Walsh Publishers
www.walshpublishers.com

Printed in the United States of America
ISBN: 978-1-54391-590-7 (hardback)

Book layout by Darlene Swanson • www.van-garde.com

Table of Contents

Acknowledgements

I WANT TO thank and acknowledge those who support my creative projects. My wife Janet who has always been in my corner when it comes to my creative projects. Starting with my acoustic solo piano music CD, *Castle of Dreams*, without which the completion of this book series may have never come to pass. Janet worked with me and is co-author of the first book in the series, "*Castle of Dreams and the Dragon Princess*".

A special thank you to, Kimberly Hofstetter, my special project advisory editor. Thanks to her input and advice, the twenty five thousand plus words in this book keep the story connected chapter to chapter.

I also want to thank the companies I selected who helped get the book published and distributed. Bookbaby.com who designed the book cover artwork and distributed the book and e-book on the internet.

My thanks to Darlene Swanson at van-garde.com for the internal book layout.

Finally, my thanks goes to you, the reader. I hope you enjoy this book of fantasy and imagination. If you are a creative person I hope that nothing stands in the way of you completing your projects. Every project you complete may not earn you millions of dollars, but the satisfaction of completing something can make you proud that you did it.

Chapter 1

Tunnel to the Past

THE MORNING SUN rose to begin a new day on a small island in the Atlantic not far from the larger island of Ireland. It was spring. The air was calm this morning except for an occasional breeze blowing from the south. As the sun rose higher in the sky, the morning dew on the grass glistened as the sun beams crossed each blade of grass.

A shepherd boy, young Thomas McGill, was tending a small flock of sheep. Just over a small rise was a very large tree which stood a few hundred yards from an ancient castle wall. As Thomas approached the tree, he noticed a kaleidoscope of butterflies fluttering in the tall grass. Thomas approached the butterflies, and as he did, they flew away from him in the direction of the very large tree.

There were at least a dozen Peacock butterflies, with their prominent red wings and superbly colored large eyespots, those were easy to spot. He noticed tortoiseshell butterflies which were the most common of the colorful butterflies in this area. Also a group of three, even more common white butterflies, were flying close to each other.

Off to the right of this swarm was a single blue butterfly fluttering closer to the tree than the rest of them. This was the first time that Thomas had ever seen a blue butterfly. He was fascinated and wanted to get a closer look. He looked back to his sheep to check if they were all together, then he turned and began to walk up to get a better look at the blue butterfly. At first the butterfly flew away from him when a slight breeze blew and lifted the butterfly much higher in the sky. Thomas watched as the breeze pushed the butterfly up and down and farther away from him. The blue butterfly appeared to be trying to fly in the direction of the tree, fighting against the breeze that was blowing it in the opposite direction.

As Thomas got closer to the tree himself, he noticed a large opening at the base, large enough for him to stand in. He watched as the butterfly flew into the opening. Thomas approached, poked his head into the opening and looked around for the butterfly, but it was too dark to see it.

Pulling his head out from the tree's opening for a moment, Thomas looked back again to check on his flock of sheep. They were grazing and grouped together so he turned back to the opening in the base of the tree and stepped inside.

A strange sensation came over him. Feeling a little dizzy, he lost his balance and began to fall. Thomas quickly reached up to grab anything he could to stop from falling, but just as he grabbed a branch, his feet were no longer touching the ground beneath him.

Hanging there, he looked down and could see a light and what appeared to be a ledge below. Thomas was losing his grip, so he swung himself over, let go of the branch, and landed on the ledge, just a few feet from a drop that seem to go down a hundred feet.

Still feeling a little strange, and now scared, Thomas stood to look down the deep hole. He bent down, picked up a small stone and dropped it into the pit. A few seconds went by before he heard the stone hit the bottom with the sound of a splash. "*Water*", he thought, *"perhaps this is an old well? But how am I to get out of here?"* He thought to himself.

His father had gone into the village this morning for supplies, and when he returned, he would not be able to find Thomas. Looking around, Thomas was trying to think of a way out. Fortunately there was enough light for him to see, but where was the light coming from? Some of the light was coming from above where he was standing just moments before, shining down fifteen or twenty feet above him. "*Could I climb back up to the top?*" He wondered. Moving to the edge of the wall, he attempted to climb it, but there was nothing to hold on to. Thomas made several attempts, but after climbing a few feet up he would always fall back to the ledge.

As his eyes began to adjust more to the limited amount of light, he noticed a lever on the wall. Pulling it down he could hear movement, sounds, and then the wall began to shake. Dirt from the wall started falling on and around him. Thomas dropped to the ledge floor in fear. In a few moments the dust and dirt had settled. Now it was even lighter in the area where he was lying and he looked in the direction of the beam of light shining through the dust to see a tunnel now in front of him.

Standing up, Thomas brushed himself off and took a few steps into the tunnel opening. On the wall he could see rows of torches on both sides. Some were lit which provided plenty of light to see a clear pathway down the tunnel.

"What is this place?" Thomas thought. *"Perhaps an ancient underground passage to the old castle?"* Thomas was scared, but knowing that he had no other choice he had to follow the tunnel to see

where it would lead. After walking a few hundred feet, the tunnel came to a fork. *"What to do next?"* Thomas could go either left or right. Thomas remembered a line from a book he had once read, *"Left is death right is right."* That made it easy for Thomas to decide what to do next, so he started down the tunnel to the right.

After another 100 feet or so, he could see a door. It was a very old-looking door, from the middle ages. Fear started to well up inside of him again. *"What if I try to open it and the walls come crashing in around me again!"* Thomas thought.

But he felt as if he had no choice, so he tried to open the door. With his shoulder against it and pushing hard with his legs, the door opened a crack and with a few more pushes he had opened it completely into a room.

Thomas's eyes opened wide. There was a lot of light in this room, and to his surprise a group of men dressed in medieval garments now stared back at him.

Speechless, Thomas looked at the men and the men looked back at him. Several of the men spoke at once, *"Where did you come from? Who are you? How did you get in here?"*

Thomas quietly replied, *"Well I fell through the ground and then followed the tunnel to here."*

Another man remarked, *"What kind of clothes are you wearing lad?"*

Thomas was thinking the same thing about the men sitting around the table in the middle of the room.

A third man spoke up, *"I think we better take you to see Sir Lawrence, come with me boy."*

The man stood up and started toward Thomas. Thomas stepped back to avoid the man reaching to grab him.

"Come with me, it will be alright," the man said gently. Thomas followed the man out of the room through the doorway on the other side of the room, and up the stairs. They then walked across a breezeway overlooking a field some twenty five feet below the castle wall.

CHAPTER TWO

Where Am I?

THE KNIGHT LEADING Thomas to meet with Sir Lawrence entered a chamber and addressed the man inside. *"Sir Lawrence, this boy found his way into the secret chambers and the Knights meeting room, I thought that you might want to have a word with him."*

Sir Lawrence looked up from his desk directly at the boy, *"Your majesty. What did you say Sir Michael?"* Sir Lawrence was puzzled, at first glance the boy looked exactly like Prince Samuel, except for his clothes, which Sir Lawrence took better notice of after staring at him for a moment.

Sir Michael spoke, *"The boy was found in the Knights meeting room. He says he got there using the secret tunnel passageway."*

Sir Lawrence looked awestruck. *"The resemblance is remarkable, why you look just like the prince!"*

Sir Michael turned Thomas around to face him. *"Why yes he does! How did I not see this before?"* Sir Michael exclaimed.

Sir Lawrence addressed Thomas, *"What is your name boy?"*

"I'm Thomas, the shepherd's son. Where am I, and why are you all dressed like that?" Thomas replied.

Sir Lawrence responded, *"Could say the same thing about you boy, what are you wearing?"* Thomas was dressed in blue jeans, sneakers and a Beatles tee shirt.

It was at that moment that Prince Samuel entered Sir Lawrence's quarters.

Prince Samuel, the only son of King James, now age thirteen was coming for his fencing lesson. Samuel spoke, *"Sir Lawrence, my apologies for my lateness."* Prince Samuel looked to his left, saw Thomas, and thought he was staring into a looking glass.

Samuel and Thomas's eyes locked on to each other, and at the same time, they looked each other over from head to toe. Thomas stood still as Prince Samuel walked around him, observing every aspect of his person.

"Who are you?" Samuel asked. Thomas did not reply at first, but then said boldly, *"I'm Thomas, the shepherd's son."*

Samuel asked again, *"Where did you get those garments?"*

Thomas replied, *"In the village shops, at the mall."*

Samuel asked, *"What's a m-a-l-l?"*

Sir Lawrence interrupted them, knowing that this conversation could go on for hours. *"I know the shepherd's son and you're not him boy, so tell us the truth. Who are you and how did you get into the Knights chambers?"* Thomas, now feeling nervous and upset at having been called a liar, raised his voice, *"I'm Thomas, and my father runs a sheep farm. I was watching a small flock this morning out on the hill near that big old tree. I was close to the ancient castle wall when I fell through an old well or something. At the bottom of the well, I found and followed the tunnel and now I'm here."*

"Ok boy, show us," Sir Lawrence replied coldly.

They all turned and left Sir Lawrence's chambers and headed out to the giant tree on the west side of the castle.

As they walked, Samuel again began to ask Thomas questions about his clothes and such. Thomas was still in a daze and trying to understand what was happening. He could not figure out all of the strange things he was seeing around him.

The ancient castle had come alive. Everyone was dressed in medieval attire, and the castle courtyard was full of people. There were wagons filled with hay, chickens running about and knights in full body armor standing guard at the gates and on the castle walls.

It took a short while to walk through the castle and out the west gate to where the giant tree stood. The field and view from here looked the same to Thomas as before he fell. The tree had the same large opening in its base large enough for a boy to stand in. But something was different. Where were the sheep Thomas was minding? The swarm of butterflies?

When they were a few feet from the tree, Thomas started to feel strange and dizzy. All of a sudden, he collapsed and fell to the ground.

"Sir Lawrence, the boy has collapsed!" shouted Sir Michael. Sir Lawrence turned back to see Samuel kneeling over Thomas.

"Let's take him back to the castle," Sir Lawrence said, *"and call the physician."*

Samuel stated, *"No, take him to my chambers."* Sir Michael picked Thomas up and carried him back to the castle. Sir Lawrence then went to the King to inform him.

The King and the physician arrived at Prince Samuel's chamber at the same time. They both looked at Thomas, amazed by the resemblance.

Sir Lawrence explained to the King as much as he could about the sudden appearance of the boy in the Knights meeting room.

The physician examined Thomas, but he was still unconscious. The physician noticed a bump on the back of the boy's head and could only recommend that someone call him when the boy awoke. Thomas did not wake until the next morning.

It was early, the roosters were crowing and Megan had snuck into Prince Samuel's chambers to see if he could spend some time with her to-day. Unaware that Prince Samuel had not slept in his chamber bed that night, she attempted to wake Thomas, thinking that he was Samuel.

Megan took a feather from the desk and started to brush it against what she thought was Samuel's cheek. By reaction, Thomas reached up with his hand to chase away whatever might be crawling on his face. Megan brushed the feather against his face again. Thomas opened his eyes and saw Megan. Sitting up quickly he stammered, *"Wh-, who are you…where am I?"*

Megan replied, *"It's me silly, and you're warm in your bed. It's a beautiful morning and I was hop-*

ing we could go for a walk and spend some time to-gether today? Were you dreaming? Were you dreaming of me?" Thomas sat up and looked around. "Where am I?" Thomas looked at Megan, "and who are you?" he asked again.

Just then, Prince Samuel came into his chamber and saw Megan next to Thomas. "That's Megan" he answered simply. Megan, hearing Samuel's voice from across the room, she turned and saw Samuel. Then she turned back to look at Thomas, flew off the bed and ran to Prince Samuel.

Megan exclaimed, "Who is that?! I thought it was you!"

Prince Samuel spoke, "Well that is what we are trying to find out. He says his name is Thomas and that he is the shepherd's son."

Megan said, "I know the shepherd's son and that is not him! He looks just like you, he could be your twin!"

"Yes, except for the big bump on the back of his head, he could be my twin," Prince Samuel laughed.

Thomas raised his hand to his head to feel the lump on the back of his head. *"Ouch,"* he muttered as he touched it. Prince Samuel asked Megan to go get the physician so he could have a look at Thomas now that he was awake, and she went off to fetch him. Samuel and Thomas spent more time talking while they waited for the physician to arrive.

When the physician came in, he looked Thomas over but could find nothing wrong with him other than the large bump on the back of his head. He said it would take a few days for the bump on his head to go down, but he would be fine. After the physician was finished the examination, Samuel invited Thomas to the banquet hall for breakfast.

CHAPTER 3

Finding the Castle Dungeon

MEGAN RAN BACK to her quarters to tell her mother the events of the morning. It was still early and her mother was busy with her work. Eleanor was the head chambermaid to the Queen and had been so for many years before both Samuel and Megan were born.

The King and Queen had already gone down to the hall for breakfast. Megan found her mother in the Queen's chambers.

Megan asked, *"Mother, does Samuel have a twin?"* Eleanor turned to Megan, *"What on earth are you talking about?"*

"Prince Samuel, there is a boy that looks just like him, and he was sleeping in his bed and..." Megan

realized that she had just said something that she should not have said, stopped talking, and then finished with, *"well the boy looks just like the prince."*

Eleanor heard every word that Megan said and instantly replied in a stern voice, *"Megan I've told you time and time again that you cannot be sneaking off to the prince's chambers like that. If the king finds out he will be furious. We are not royalty, we cannot go around pretending to be something we are not. Our job is to serve the royal family and that is all."*

Eleanor shook her head and continued more gently, *"Now that you are older and coming of age, we have to keep our distance. It was quite different when the both of you were younger. The queen did not mind the two of you playing together, but now things are not the same."* Eleanor looked away sadly, *"We will talk about this more at another time, now off with you and finish your morning chores."*

Megan left the room and headed off to start her morning chores. Since her mother had to manage all of the cleaning and caretaking of the Queen's things, Megan was tasked with managing the daily chores for her mother and herself. Cleaning their quarters, laundry and dishes were all part of the normal routine that Megan had to tend to.

As Megan went about cleaning up, she could not help thinking about Thomas. Where did he come from and why was he saying he was the shepherd's son? Why was he dressed in those unusual garments? How did he get into the Knights' quarters? Most of all, why did he look so much like the prince?

I have to find out more, she thought to herself, *I need to speak with Samuel and Thomas.* Megan stopped sweeping, placed the broom back in its normal place, and headed out to look for Samuel.

She knew that Samuel would still be eating breakfast. She snuck up to the royal dining hall to try and get the prince's attention. Luckily, Samuel noticed her peering around a pillar. He took another sip of water from his goblet and then excused himself from the table.

Megan moved back into the hallway just outside the royal dining room and Samuel met her. *"What are you doing here?"* Samuel asked. Megan replied, *"I had to see you, did you find out anything new about how Thomas found his way to the Knights chambers?"*

"No!" Samuel replied exasperated, *"he keeps telling the same story over and over again, my father and mother don't know what to think of this."*

"We should meet out by the tree before dinner to see if we can figure this out," Megan suggested. Samuel agreed, they would meet out by the tree on the west side of the castle that evening.

The sun was hovering low in the sky when Samuel, Megan and Thomas met out by the large tree a few hundred yards from the west castle wall. Samuel and Megan were anxious to discover how Thomas got into the castle. Samuel turned to Thomas, *"Tell me exactly what happened and how you were able to get into the castle from here."*

Thomas replied and told them that he was watching his sheep when he saw a swarm of butterflies near the tree and wanted to get a closer look. Thomas told them of the one blue butterfly that flew into the opening at the base of the tree and how he went inside to investigate. Then the ground opened up beneath him and he dropped to the ledge below and followed the tunnel into the castle.

Samuel walked toward the opening in the tree and peered in. Looking down he saw the hole and the ledge below. Megan stepped forward and looked into the tree's opening as well. Thomas pointed to the branch as he explained again how the ground opened up from under him and he grabbed the branch and swung to the ledge below. Samuel looked up and saw the branch Thomas was speaking of, than looking down he saw the ledge below.

In a bold move, Samuel jumped up to the branch, grabbed it, swung himself over and landed on the ledge below. Sure enough, he saw the tunnel entrance. Thomas followed him without hesitation.

Megan cried out, *"Samuel what are you doing?"* Samuel replied, *"I had to see for myself. Come on, you can do it, just grab that branch and swing yourself over to the ledge."*

Megan was a little scared, but did not want to be left behind so she grabbed the branch and in a few swings, she landed on the ledge next to Samuel and Thomas.

"Let's go," Samuel said, *"and we'll see where this leads."* The tunnel was still dimly lit by a few torches. Samuel grabbed one of the torches and proceeded down the tunnel, lighting the other torches as he went to provide more light.

When the three of them came to the intersection where the tunnel split, Thomas told them that he went to the right and did not know where the left fork led to.

Samuel said, *"Well then let's see where it takes us, since we know the right path takes us to the Knights meeting room."* Samuel, leading the way, started down the left tunnel path. After a hundred feet or so, they came to a solid door. A door with no windows. Samuel pulled up the door handle and pushed the door open. A rush of foul warm air hit him in the face. The smell was not pleasant. The room was very dark. There were rows of doors on the left and right, four doors on each side. Each door had a small window at the top. At the end of the row of doors was another door. They moved toward it. When they reached it, Samuel again lifted the handle and pushed the door open into a large room.

Samuel remarked, *"This is the dungeon! I have never been down here before. I did not believe we actually had one! It has not been used for a very long time."*

Megan spoke up, *"Let's get out of here, this is just awful."* Just then a rat ran past them and Megan screamed, *"Let's get out of here, hurry!"*

There was a door on the other side of the room, the three of them ran toward it, this time Thomas lifted the door handle and pulled the door toward him. There was a flight of stairs leading upward. The three of them dashed out from the dungeon and headed up the stairs. A slight breeze of fresh air blew past them as they reached the top of the steps.

Megan remarked, *"I'm glad to be out of that place, do you think they tortured people down there?"* *"Perhaps a long time ago, but we have not been at war with anyone for many years,"* Samuel said.

Having found the tunnel, this proved to Samuel and Megan that Thomas had been telling the truth of how he got into the castle, but it did not explain why he looked so much like the prince or the strange clothes he was wearing.

CHAPTER 4

Dining with the King and Queen

THE SUN WAS setting now and Prince Samuel knew that it was time for dinner. He headed straight to the banquet hall. Thomas went with him while Megan headed back to her chamber to eat with her mother.

The hall was a grand room, with a long wooden table in the middle. The table was twelve feet in length and very wide. The King sat at the head of the table while the Queen sat at the other end. The royal court was normally in attendance, but not this night.

There were several Knights there, the first Knight Sir Lawrence, and Sir Michael. One of the Queen's brothers, Sir John and the royal physician.

There were two other shorter tables in the room as well. One on either side of the main table, ten feet in length. Most of the other knights who were not standing guard would be seated at one or the other of these tables. In all, the hall could hold fifty to sixty people.

When there were feasts, they required fifteen to twenty servants and cooks to serve the royals. Such times would be for visiting guests from other lands, but this was not one of those occasions.

The word had been spreading throughout the castle of the appearance of the strange boy who looked like the prince. Most people were discussing this excitedly when Thomas and Samuel entered the dining hall. When they did, all eyes turned to Thomas. The whispers were many. Some thought that he might be the son of the king's brother and that is why he looked so much like Prince Samuel.

The ringing of the dinner bell sounded to announce that dinner was about to be served. With the sound of the bell, everyone began to take their places.

Missing from her place at the main table was Lady Elizabeth, second cousin to the King. Lady Elizabeth was not your typical lady of the King's court. She was more of a psychic, some thought she was in fact a witch. She could see into the future and predict events. She knew the past and the history of the kingdom better than anyone.

Lady Elizabeth had a small cottage deep in the woods, just off the south road to the castle. The cottage was full of books stacked on shelves and piled around a table in the center of the main room. There were vials of potions on the mantel just above a large kettle that hung in the fireplace.

Lady Elizabeth always dressed in flowing, multicolored garments. She walked with a tall staff that had many engraved carvings of dragons and butterflies. A very strange combination one might think.

The servants began serving the meal. This evening, like most other meals, lamb and potatoes were the main course. Large bowls of bread were spread on the tables as bread was always a big part of every meal, and no meal would be complete without wine.

Halfway through the dinner, Lady Elizabeth entered the hall and all heads turned to watch her as she walked straight up to Thomas. She stared at him for a moment, then she turned to the King and spoke, *"The boy must go back, you must send him back at once. He is a sign, a sign from the future. It is written in the legend. His coming has been foreseen, the kingdom is in danger."*

The King did not hear a word that Lady Elizabeth had spoken, nor was he aware she had entered the hall. He was deep in conversation with Sir Lawrence who was sitting to his left.

Elizabeth thumped her walking staff loudly on the ground to get the King's attention and repeated her warning, *"The boy must go back, you must send him back at once. It is written in the legend. His coming has been foreseen, the kingdom is in danger."*

The whole room went silent, the King looked at Elizabeth and replied, *"What are you going on about woman?"*

Elizabeth cried, *"The boy, he must go back, the legend!"* The King stated, *"We are not sure who he is or how he got here."* Elizabeth was holding an ancient book and dropped it in front of the King. A page with a dark drawing of dragons and fire showing the destruction of the castle lay before him.

The King studied the drawing for a few moments, the room had gone completely quiet. He realized it was the legend his father and grandfather had told him about many years ago. King James stood, picked up the book and looked at Sir Lawrence. Sir Lawrence stood as the King started walking toward Thomas. The King grabbed Thomas by the collar as he passed him and dragged him out of the hall with him.

All of the King's court followed close behind. The King headed straight for the war room and slammed the ancient book on the table. Lady Elizabeth stood on his left. The knights who had followed the King from the hall took their places at the war table.

On the table was a map of the kingdom. The line of defenses and many models and figures of men were lined up on the model of the castle and its walls. Models of dragons were positioned on the mountain ranges.

The King looked up, everyone was in their rightful place at the war table, and he spoke. *"We must make our preparations. We will not be sure where the threat will come from so we will need to be ready for anything from any direction."*

"Lady Elizabeth you must be sure, if this is true you must begin to find a way for us to return the boy from wherever it is that he came from."

Lady Elizabeth picked up the ancient book from in front of the King, turned to Thomas and said, *"You must come with me back to my cottage so we can determine how you got here and how to send you back."*

CHAPTER 5

Preparations for the Unknown

MEGAN RAN BACK to her chambers. Her mother was stitching a garment when she came into the room. Megan had been eavesdropping on the war counsel's meeting. Samuel had once shown her a way to get to one of the balconies that overlooked the war room chamber. From there you could see and hear all that went on without being detected as long as you remained quiet and kept your head down.

"*Mother, the King has called the war counsel together. It has something to do with the boy Thomas who was discovered in the Knights chambers yesterday.*"

Megan's mother responded, *"What are you going on about child? You need to stay clear of what is going on with such things or we could find ourselves living in the village and not here in the castle."*

Megan murmured to herself, *"You never listen to me."* She thought, *"Something mysterious is going on, there is something about an ancient legend with dragons and fire...the Castle and everyone in it could be in danger because of this boy!"* Megan stormed out of the room and headed toward Prince Samuel's chambers to see what else she could find out.

It was dark now. Torches lit the castle corridors as Megan made her way to Prince Samuel's chamber. She did not find him there. She was not sure where to look next, perhaps he was still in the war room? Megan heard someone approaching, so she quickly dashed behind one of the pillars. It was Sir Lawrence, Sir Michael and two other knights. *"You two stand guard here to protect the prince."* Sir Lawrence pointed to two guards that Megan did not know. The guards were dressed in full armor, and did as they were ordered positioning themselves near Prince Samuel's chamber door.

When the guards were not looking, Megan headed down the hall in the other direction, still looking for Prince Samuel. The moon was high in the sky this night and as Megan crossed over the breezeway, the moon lit up the courtyard below. She spotted Samuel and yelled down to him, *"Samuel, where are you going?"* Samuel turned and looked up at her. He motioned for her to come down and meet him at the rear gate.

In a few minutes, Megan had made her way down to the courtyard and there near the rear gate stood Samuel. *"Where are you going?"* Megan asked.

Samuel replied, *"I am headed to Lady Elizabeth's cottage to see Thomas. I need to find out more about the legend and why my father is so worried. He put the Castle Knights on high alert. He put two guards at my chamber door and ordered me to stay in my room. You should go back to your chambers!"*

Megan remarked, *"Yes I know, I saw the guards. How did you get out of your room?"*

"I climbed out of my window like I did in the past to come see you when we were little. Now go back to your chamber this is too risky for you."

Megan replied, *"No, I'm coming with you."*

The two of them looked around to check that the coast was clear and then snuck out the rear gate.

The cottage was a few miles away from the castle and it took a while to get there. The darkness of the night made it a little more difficult to manage, but they had the advantage of a clear sky and a full moon. Samuel was wearing his sword. Megan walking alongside of him every step of the way and they talked to each other as they went.

Samuel tried to explain to Megan as much as he knew about the ancient legend, stories he was told at bedtime by his grandfather. *"This is what my grandfather told me years ago when I was little,"* Samuel started to explain. *"There is a legend regarding the mountains to the north. In those mountains lived the dragons of the island. When people first came to the island, the dragons would fly down unexpectedly and carry off anyone not under cover.*

It did not matter if you were peasant or noble. If you were out in the open when the dragons were in the sky you could be snatched up in a flash."

Samuel went on, *"My ancestors decided to go to the mountains to seek out the dragons. It takes a week or more to journey to those mountains. A hundred men went and only one returned. My great, great, great grandfather. He was just a boy at the time. He returned with the head of one of the dragons and the villagers made him the King of the land. That is when he decreed that a castle should be built to protect the villagers."*

"It took many years to build the castle and there were many more expeditions to the mountain range to find the dragons' nest and destroy it. A generation passed. A prince and princess were born, twins. One day, the two of them were out playing by the ancient tree when a thunderstorm came up suddenly. When the storm passed, the princess was gone. Everyone thought that a dragon had snatched her up and carried her off to the mountains.

The King sent his Knights to find her. The kingdom despaired when they returned without having found the young princess. Years passed and each year expeditions would be sent out to look for her. The queen became ill and died, some say of a broken heart. When the King died after ten years of searching, the King's son took the throne. He saw no point to continue the expeditions so he stopped sending Knights out to find his sister."

"For the first few years after the princess disappeared, the dragons still came, snatching up sheep, goats and sometimes people. The King had the builders construct towers first, complete with bells. The King posted guards in each of the towers to watch the skies for the approaching dragons. When a dragon was sighted, the guards would sound the bells to warn the villagers to take cover. The entire castle was then fitted with secret passageways, one on every side: north, south, east and west. All the passageways were accessible by the villagers to use so they could take cover from the dragons."

"Then one day the dragons just stopped appearing. No one knows why. That is when the legend came about. One day the dragons would reappear and destroy the castle and village...and burn everything to the ground," Samuel finished speaking and Megan remained silent as she reflected on the tale of the legend.

Megan and Samuel turned the final corner on the path to Lady Elizabeth's cottage. The cottage was nestled in a small grove. There were a few torches lit on the path to the front door. There was a well built from stone with a small wooden roof for fresh water. The well was just a few feet from the front door off to the left. The window shutters were all closed, but you could see bits of light sneaking out from the cracks in the shutters.

Samuel approached the door and knocked. A voice came from inside, *"Who's there?"*

Samuel replied, *"Lady Elizabeth, it is Prince Samuel, I've come to speak with you."* Lady Elizabeth swiftly opened the door and ushered Prince Samuel and Megan inside.

CHAPTER 6
Lady Elizabeth's Cottage / The Reading

LADY ELIZABETH SPOKE, *"I was expecting you both, my lord, would you like a spot of tea?"*

"No thank you" said Samuel and Megan together.

Thomas was sitting over by the fireplace when Samuel and Megan entered the cottage. Thomas rose to his feet as Lady Elizabeth welcomed her visitors.

Lady Elizabeth had many candles burning in the cottage. There were books and papers scattered everywhere. A round table was in the middle of the room and the fireplace was on the back wall with a line of lit candles on the mantel. A few books were open on the table. Samuel noticed a large book in the middle of the table. It was opened to a page with a drawing of the castle on fire. This was the same picture that Lady Elizabeth had shown the King in the dining hall.

Samuel moved toward the table to get a better look. He only had a chance to glance at it when Lady Elizabeth first showed it to the King. Lady Elizabeth was talking to Megan as Samuel studied the drawing closely. Thomas moved toward Samuel now, looking down at the same drawing as well.

The drawing was very detailed, each of the castle towers appeared to be ablaze in fire. The courtyard was filled with wagons of hay and animals laying on the ground beside them. A line of peasants were throwing buckets of water, desperately trying to put out the fires that engulfed the castle. The sky above the castle was full of dragons shooting streams of fire at the whole scene below.

Samuel spoke, *"What are these books telling you? Is the legend true? Are the dragons coming back to destroy the castle?"*

Lady Elizabeth answered, *"From what I have seen and read, the prophecy is about to unfold."* She walked over to a smaller table where there was a crystal ball. The ball was aglow as Lady Elizabeth sat down at the table. Megan, Samuel and Thomas all walked over to get a closer look. Silence filled the room.

The three of them waited for Lady Elizabeth to speak. She turned to her right and opened a small book. *"Someone bring me my tea,"* she asked.

Megan turned, noticed a cup on the table, and brought it to her. Lady Elizabeth took the cup and dumped the tea on the floor. Then, she began looking back and forth between the cup and the book, attempting to interpret the tea leaf patterns that remained in the cup.

"My wand, someone hand me my wand," she muttered. Samuel handed her the wand that was lying next to the crystal ball. Lady Elizabeth seemed to be in deep concentration. Now holding the cup in her left hand, and her wand in her right, she motioned the wand over the cup.

"Reveal!" The remaining leaves began to change positions inside the cup, some flying out and others repositioning themselves to form a new image.

The tea leaves now appeared in the shape of a dragon. *"Thomas come here,"* Lady Elizabeth ordered. *"Take that other cup and pour yourself a cup of tea."*

Thomas replied, *"I don't drink tea."*

"Do it..." Elizabeth ordered again, *"pour a cup of tea."*

Thomas picked up the empty cup, reached for the tea kettle and poured himself a cup of tea. *"Now drink,"* Elizabeth insisted. Thomas put the cup to his mouth and began sipping at the tea. His face turned to disgust as the smell and taste permeated his nose and lips.

Elizabeth then took the cup from Thomas and poured the remaining tea on the floor. She placed his cup next to hers and looked at the shapes of the remaining tea leaves in Thomas's cup. Once again, she continued referring back to the book, turning pages and looking at the tea leaves in each cup.

"What does it mean?" Megan asked, *"What do you see?"* Elizabeth did not reply. Instead, she turned to Thomas and asked, *"When is your birthday?"*

Thomas replied, *"November 15"*.

"The year, what year?" she asked harshly.

"1953..." he replied in fear.

Samuel and Megan were puzzled by his response. There was no such year as 1953.

"Samuel hand me that deck of cards from the small table," Elizabeth asked. Samuel walked over to the small table and gathered up the cards that were there and brought them over to Lady Elizabeth.

Elizabeth began to shuffle the deck and after a few moments, she put the cards down on the table in front of Thomas. *"Thomas,"* she said, *"Make three piles from this deck of cards."* Thomas did as she asked, and separated the deck of cards into three piles.

Elizabeth then gathered up the three piles into one pile again. She took the top card from the new single pile and placed a card, one at a time, onto the table in front of them. When she was finished dealing out the cards, they formed a pattern on the table, a Celtic Cross.

The Four of Cups was the first card drawn from the deck. The picture on the card was that of a young boy, sitting against a tree. Three gold cups upright in front of him, and one cup floating before him as if being handed to him by an invisible force. Thomas stared at the card, wondering if this card symbolized him, sitting by the large tree that brought him to this place and time.

Next, a card with the word Judgement written in sand script at the bottom. The picture was what appeared to be an angel blowing a trumpet. An eerie feeling overcame Thomas, Samuel and Megan as they all peered down at the Judgement card. What could this mean? Were they about to witness the unfolding of the legend? Who was to be judged? And for what?

The third card was placed on the table, the Seven of Wands. A picture of a man standing in a doorway holding a wand, and surrounded by six other wands. What was he guarding? What was he protecting? Will he be victorious against whatever danger is approaching?

Elizabeth looked over each of the cards on the table. She drew the fourth card from the deck and placed it below the Seven of Wands. It was the Knight of Wands.

Samuel saw himself in this card. A Knight on horseback ready to take action, ready to defend the castle and the people he loves. The next card drawn by Elizabeth was placed to the left of the Judgement card. It was the Ace of Cups. This was a beautifully colored card with a golden chalice in the center floating on water, with an eye staring down at the cup. The phases of the moon formed a semi-circle over the eye.

Megan, looking at this card, and began to develop a sense of hope that everything would work out in the end. Her fears were calmed for a moment, as the feeling spread through her that they would get through whatever was to come. She also sensed that the relationship between her, Samuel and now Thomas, would be a lasting friendship.

The next card was placed above the Judgement card, the Eight of Pentacles. This card depicted a young boy sitting at a desk, working with, or studying, a pentacle. The hour appeared to be late, there were candles lit near the desk as the young boy focused on his work. Megan's mind started to wander, could she possibly learn how to do all the things that Elizabeth was doing?

The final card to make up the pattern of the Celtic Cross was positioned to the right of the Judgement card, the Eight of Cups. A young man stands with his back to eight cups. Some of the cups stand upright in the grass, while some have fallen over. A full moon is in the sky in front of him. He has a staff in hand and there is a mountain range off in the distance. Thomas looked intently at this card, wondering what lay ahead of him. He was too afraid to say anything, so he remained silent.

Samuel was thinking of the dragons that the legend spoke of, in the distant mountains far from the castle. *What was his role going to be in all of this?*

Megan asked, "What does this all mean?"

Lady Elizabeth was now convinced after laying out the cards. She said, *"The legend is about to come true, we must prepare and inform the King to make ready."* Elizabeth rose from the card table and walked toward the front door. Taking her shawl and walking cane, she opened the door, turned to the children and motioned them to follow.

Samuel, Thomas and Megan gathered their things and followed behind her.

Chapter 7

"Making Ready"

As Elizabeth and the children made their way back to the castle, it was very late. The moon was high in the sky earlier, but now was lower and did not provide much light. The wind was blowing stronger and clouds were moving in from the mountain range.

The children had been gone for hours and Eleanor had been worried about the whereabouts of her daughter after dinner. After an hour, Eleanor could not wait any longer for Megan to appear and so she went to the Queen to ask if she had seen Megan.

Eleanor entered the Queens chambers timidly. *"My lady, I am sorry to bother you, but have you*

seen Megan? I have not seen her since sundown."
The Queen responded quickly, "No, I have not."

"Could we perhaps ask the prince if he has seen her?"

The Queen sighed, "He has not seen her, the
King sent the prince to his room right after dinner
and placed two knights at his door to watch him."

Eleanor asked more urgently, "Please, my lady,
can we ask him?"

The Queen sighed again, but got up and left her
chamber. They went out into the hallway, headed
toward Prince Samuel's room. As they approached,
the knights on guard bowed to the Queen.

"Good Evening, my lady," one of the guards
said as the other asked, "Is everything alright?"

"Yes", the Queen answered, "I need to speak to
my son."

"Of course," the first guard replied.

The Queen entered the prince's chamber calling his name, "Samuel!" The room was very large,
the prince's bed was 20 feet or so from the room's
front door. There were two large windows to the
right as you entered and a small table and two

chairs set up in front of them. The queen called his name again, *"Samuel!"* and then puzzled, *"Samuel...?"*

There was no reply and the Queen realized that Samuel was not in his room. Eleanor had wandered over to the small table and noticed a rope hanging out one of the windows in Samuel's chamber.

"Your majesty, I don't think he is here." She said as she pulled up the rope from the window. The Queen turned to Eleanor and her eyes widened as she noticed the rope in the woman's hand.

Eleanor spoke again, *"Where do you think he was off to?"*

The Queen paused for a moment, then spoke, *"I think I know where we can find them. My guess would be that they have gone off to Lady Elizabeth's cottage."*

The Queen and Eleanor took leave of Prince Samuel's chambers and as the Queen walked passed the knights on duty, she ordered them to follow her. Heading for the war room on the other side of the castle, she was sure she would find the King there.

Lady Elizabeth and the children had managed to make their way back to the castle and were coming up to the south gate still a few hundred yards away.

As the Queen entered the war room, she addressed the King, *"Samuel is not in his room, and we believe he has gone to Elizabeth's cottage. We need to send someone after him."*

The King looked up from the war counsel table, *"What do you mean he is not in his room? I have two guards watching him."* The King now looking passed the queen, and noticed the two knights standing behind her, the same knights he had assigned to guard the prince.

One knight spoke up, *"Your majesty it appears that he climbed down a rope out the window of his chamber to the courtyard."* The King just shook his head and then ordered the men to get his horse ready to ride.

"I'll go get him, don't worry my Queen." The King put his hand on the Queen's shoulders as he spoke. Everyone then followed the King as he ex-

ited the war room. As the King, Queen, Eleanor and a few knights headed out toward the stables, they ran into Sir Lawrence.

"My lord, where are you going?" asked Sir Lawrence concernedly.

The King replied, *"Apparently the prince has snuck out of his chambers and wandered off to see Lady Elizabeth. I will return shortly."*

As they entered the courtyard, the Queen noticed Lady Elizabeth and the children coming in through the south gate. There were two guards escorting them. *"Your majesties,"* Elizabeth called hurriedly, *"I am convinced that the legend is about to unfold, I have completed my reading, you must prepare the castle and the people!"*

The King responded, *"Are you sure?"*

Elizabeth looked at him pleadingly, *"Yes, your highness."*

The King turned to the Queen and she nodded to him.

"We will be ready. Guards, back to your post and alert your commanders, have them meet me in

the war room. Samuel you and I will talk in the morning, now return to your chamber and this time stay there!"

At that, the guards hurried off in the direction of the castle knights' quarters. Morning was fast approaching, the moon was almost set and the sky was getting lighter.

It was not long before everyone was gathered in the war room. Samuel, Thomas and Megan were ordered to return to their chambers for the night.

The war council meeting continued until mid-morning. The council had concluded to put their plans into effect immediately. The four towers would be manned at all times, day and night like they had been centuries ago. The court scribe was drafting a notice that would be printed, distributed and posted though out the kingdom.

The post read:

Citizens of the kingdom.

We have received warning that the ancient legend and prophecy of our forefathers is come to pass. Heed the warning bells when you hear them and take cover. All able-bodied men must report to the master of arms.

Once the notice was printed, the squires were dispatched to post them in taverns and other prominent places throughout the kingdom. As soon as the notices were posted, the villagers began gathering around them. Not everyone could read, and those that could would read the notices out loud to the others gathered.

Fear was building and crowds of villagers were walking to the castle to get more information. Not everyone knew of the legend or of the prophecy. Most of the older folks knew the tale, but as stories are passed down over generations, they have a way of changing over time.

As the courtyard filled with peasants, villagers, farmers and shepherds, the guards on duty got nervous and closed the castle gates to prevent others from entering. The crowd began to get rowdy and called out for the King. More and more people gathered outside the gates of the castle, yelling and protesting to be let in.

The Queen was in her chambers reading and began to hear all of the noise going on outside. She looked out her chamber window and saw the crowds gathering, dropped her book to the floor and hurried off to notify the King.

The King was pacing the hallways of the castle when the Queen found him. She informed him of all the angry people inside and outside the castle walls.

The King hurried to the causeway to look out over the courtyard. A farmer noticed him and called out, *"Your Majesty, is it true? When is this going to happen? How can we protect ourselves?"*

The King held his arms up to quiet the crowd and then replied, *"It will be alright, all of the knights are on alert and the bells will ring to alert everyone to take cover."*

The King then looked over the other side of the causeway, down at the peasants outside of the castle walls. They were all calling out, *"Let us in, save us! Don't leave us out here!"*

The King noticed a small group trying to set up a ladder to climb over the walls. The King hurried over to the guards and ordered them to open the gates.

The Queen shouted down to the peasants below, *"We are opening the gates, we will not leave you unprotected. Please stay calm!"* The Queen hurried over to where the King was near the main gate. *"My lord, we will have to make provisions for those who want to stay in the castle."*

With that the King called over the castle guards and directed them to set up areas for those who wanted to stay within the castle walls. Hundreds more people made their way into the courtyard. It was getting extremely crowded. Sir Lawrence came into the courtyard, saw the chaos and took charge. Along with the guards, he was able to settle things down after a few hours. Once things had quieted, the King came out to the causeway again to address the people.

The King began, *"Good people, I know that some of you are scared and do not understand the meaning of the notice that was posted. The notice was posted as a precaution. We have received evidence that the ancient prophecy is about to come true. We do not know when this will happen. I must ask you all to stay calm and we will do what we can to keep you informed and protect you."*

At that, someone from the crowd shouted, *"Does this have to do with that strange boy who appeared?"* And then others starting shouting, *"Where is he from? Why is he here? Is he a warlock? Why does he look so much like the prince?"*

Thomas had been looking out from Samuel's chamber window, and some people in the crowd turned to look up at him.

The King spoke again, *"Quiet, please, quiet! We are looking into the boy, who he is, how he arrived here and what he has to do with the legend. We do not see him as a threat but more as a messenger. Please give us time to find out more. For now it is more important that we make our preparations if the legend is about to unfold."*

The King then turned and walked off the causeway and into the castle tower. The crowd still milled about, groups of people were talking and trying to make sense of the situation. The castle guards started to organize the grounds for those who wished to remain behind.

CHAPTER 8

"First Sighting"

A FEW DAYS passed and nothing. Nothing bad happened, no dragons flew in the skies above the castle and no people or animals were missing. There were no bad storms or fire raining down from the sky.

Every day since Lady Elizabeth had told the King the legend was about to unfold, nothing had changed. In fact, the opposite was true. The weather could not have been better, there were clear skies both day and night, warm temperatures during the day and just a little cooler at night. More and more people were returning back to the village and fields. Things were getting back to normal. Was this all a false alarm?

The King had sent out patrols every day, even a small expedition to the mountain range. Ten knights volunteered to travel to the mountains to see what they could find. It took a week to ten days for them to reach the mountains and the same amount of time to return back to the castle to report.

Lady Elizabeth was still busy looking over books, crystal balls, tea leaves and meeting with the elders of the village. She wanted to know how the prophecy and legend had been passed down through the generations so she could better predict when the actual events would happen. She was very puzzled that nothing had happened but still remained convinced that her reading of the cards and tea leaves were correct. The questions still remained, when would these terrible events take place? How could they be predicted with more certainty?

Thomas was getting better accustomed to living in this time period. He was living in medieval times. There was no running water, no bathrooms, no electricity, and no TV or music players. When he was not busy, he was thinking of home. He wondered what was happening there and were they looking for him?

Thomas spent a lot of time with Samuel and Megan. They were teaching him how to do things, while he would try to explain to them how things were different and so much easier in his time.

They found themselves growing fond of each other as the first few days passed from when Thomas was first discovered in the knights meeting room.

Then something happened. A shepherd was watching over a small flock of sheep a few miles from the castle on a hillside that overlooked the mountain range in the distance. It was close to evening, the sun was setting and the evening sky was getting darker. The shepherd was making his final count of the flock before getting ready to go to his campsite to prepare something to eat.

All of a sudden, the sheep began to scatter in all directions. The shepherd's back was turned toward the mountain range and he felt a slight breeze on his neck. The sheep settled down with some coaxing from the shepherd and he continued his count. *Eighteen, nineteen, twenty...one short...*, he thought to himself.

Turning to look behind him, he saw there were no sheep behind him, the entire herd was in front of him. So he began his count again. He felt this time for sure he would count all twenty one.

Eighteen, nineteen, twenty...again he came up one short. Turning back to look around once again, he checked again that the missing sheep was not behind him. It was much darker now, there were a few clouds in the sky, and what appeared to be a very large bird or group of birds flying off in the distance toward the mountain range.

It was getting too dark to look for the lost sheep, the shepherd returned to his camping area as most of the sheep were laying down for the night. Once the sun rose in the morning the shepherd knew he could get a better count of his herd since most would still be lying in the grass or grazing in the early morning. When the sun started to rise, the shepherd was up early and counting the herd once again, but he still came up one sheep short.

The shepherd shook his head and went back to his campsite to eat and break camp so he could move the flock of sheep to another area of the hillside today. Just as he was rolling up his mat, the sheep again started stirring and scattering in all directions. The shepherd looked up into the sky just out over the horizon in the direction of the mountain range. There, about to swoop down on the herd, was a dragon.

The shepherd could not believe his eyes. He blinked hard to refocus, opened his eyes again, and yes, a dragon was about to snatch up one of the sheep into its dangling claws. The dragon's wing span was huge, extending ten feet on either side of his dark greyish green body. Its body was very muscular with scales that looked like armor. The tail extended out ten feet or so from his body, waving back and forth in the air as it plunged downward to grab an innocent sheep.

The cries of the sheep were agonizing to hear as the dragon sunk its claws into it, lifting it from the field. The dragon's mighty wings pressed harder to lift its prey into the air, gaining height and flying back toward the mountains.

The shepherd was stunned to have witnessed this, not sure what to do, what if the dragon came back? What if there was more than one dragon? What to do? There was no point in calling out for help. He was miles away from the castle. The sheep were settling down once again. He attempted to gather them up into a bunch to lead them off the hillside.

It took some time to get the flock together. Now the count was 19. Two less sheep than he had started with the day before. The shepherd decided to go to the castle to inform them of what had happened and what he saw.

It took most of the day for the shepherd to get

to the castle. Leaving the flock unattended about a mile from the castle walls, the shepherd had to leave the flock behind in an open field and continue to the castle gate on his own.

As he approached the gate he could see the knights atop the castle walls, pacing back and forth. A knight was looking out from one of the two towers on either side where the walls met. The main gate was open and two knights stood outside, checking people as they entered or left the castle courtyard.

Finally the shepherd was at the castle gate. *"I must see the King"*, he said urgently to the guard at the gate. The knight responded, *"I'm sorry no one can see the King"*. "But I saw a dragon!" cried the shepherd, *"In the hills while I was minding my flock. The dragon took two of my sheep back to the mountain range, I must tell the king!"*

At that, the stunned knight immediately led the shepherd to the war room where the King was meeting with Sir Lawrence and a few other knights.

The shepherd entered the war room and bowed to the King. *"Your majesty I have seen a dragon in the foot hills to the west, toward the mountain range.*

It swooped down right in front of me this morning and snatched up one of my sheep. Another had gone missing last evening."

The King responded, *"Are you sure, Quinn? "* The King knew the shepherd by name and had many dealings with him over the years. The castle bought his sheep's wool for clothes and many lambs for royal banquets.

"Where again were you when you saw the dragon? Show me here." The King pointed to the war table. Quinn approached the table and pointed to the area on the map where his sheep had been grazing.

The King placed a model dragon on the spot on the map where Quinn indicated. The King turned to Sir Lawrence, *"Send for my son and the boy Thomas. Have someone bring Quinn's son here as well."* Sir Lawrence turned and exited the war room to bring Thomas and Prince Samuel to the war chamber.

The King then turned back to Quinn, *"I need to ask you, how is your son? You should bring him here, but first I need you to meet the young lad who was discovered in the knights meeting room a few days ago. He claims to be your son."*

Quinn responded, *"My son is fine, he is at home with his mother. I have been out with the herd for the past week or so. My son has only been to the castle a few times, I do not see how he would have found the knights meeting room!"*

At that, Prince Samuel and Thomas entered the war room. Quinn greeted the Prince with a bow, *"Your Majesty"*. Looking back up at Thomas, he saw there was a resemblance to his son, but far from identical. Quinn's son had more reddish hair and was shorter. Thomas appeared to be more like Prince Samuel's twin.

The King spoke, *"This is the boy who claims to be your son."*

Thomas spoke up right away. *"This man is not my father, my-."*

The King interrupted, *"Easy lad, I just wanted to clear this up once and for all. This is Quinn, he is the shepherd we all know. I have had one of our knights go fetch Quinn's son so there is no mistake."*

It was not long before the knight who was sent to get Quinn's son returned with him and his mother.

Quinn's son ran to his father as soon as he entered the war room. Quinn looked down at his son as he spoke, *"Father, the notice! The notice of the legend, is it true, the stories you told me when I was younger, are the dragons really coming to eat us?"*

Quinn turned to the King. His wife was now standing next to him and hugging her husband and son. The King spoke solemnly, *"Quinn it may be best if your family stays here inside the castle until we can sort this out. Now that you have seen what you have seen, we have the confirmation we have been fearing."*

The King then turned to the knight, *"Find them some accommodations. Sir Lawrence, send for Lady Elizabeth."*

CHAPTER 9

"Dragons in the Sky"

IT WAS SEVERAL hours before Lady Elizabeth was able to get to the castle. The King had gone to dinner and then returned to the war room. When Lady Elizabeth entered the war room, she spoke immediately. *"So it's true! Quinn saw a dragon this morning! I heard the guards speaking of it as I entered the gate."*

The King responded, *"Yes, a dragon snatched up two of Quinn's sheep. Have you found out any more information in those books of yours? We need to know how we can defend the people against the dragons, I need answers and I need them now. What does that boy have to do with all of this?*

You told me the cards and tea leaves are pre-

dicting the destruction of the castle by these dragons and we need to know how many. I've dispatched ten knights to the mountain range to seek out whatever they can find. The last time men were sent to the mountain range looking for dragons only one man returned, my great, great, great grandfather."

"Your majesty," Elizabeth replied, *"I am still looking into everything I can, the answers you seek are still unclear."*

"You must find something, a spell, a potion, something to fend off the dragons from destroying the castle and village!" The King exclaimed. He motioned over the war table with the model of the castle, village and the surrounding lands. Disgusted with the situation, and with a quick motion of his hand, he dismissed Lady Elizabeth from his sight.

Elizabeth knew she had not provided the answers the king was hoping for and left the war room. With her staff in hand, she headed toward Thomas's chambers.

Thomas had been given his own room to re-side in two days after he appeared in this time. Lady Elizabeth found him sitting by the window. He was looking out and up to the sky.

"Looking for dragons, lad?" Lady Elizabeth remarked. Thomas turned and saw her standing in the doorway. He said nothing and looked back out the window. He had been thinking of his home, his family, what must they be thinking of where he was? How would they ever believe that he was in the same place as them but in another time, another dimension?

"I want to go home," Thomas remarked *"Is this really happening? I need to wake up. I miss everything."*

Elizabeth responded gently, *"I am not sure why you are here or how it came about that you are here. I would say it was very strong magic, however. It will take some very strong magic to return you to where you have come from. I believe you are the key and you must find a way to help me help you get back to your own time."*

Thomas did not answer her, he just kept staring out the window. Then in the distance, movement in the sky, like a flock of birds, but too large to be birds. The bells in the tower started ringing, dragons.

Dragons were approaching the village and fields.

The knights and people in the courtyard looked up, then scattered about looking for cover. Three dragons were flying across the sky toward the field where a small flock of sheep were grazing there. The knights on the castle walls and in the towers had the best view of the dragons. They were off in the distance, but not far. The sheep were defenseless against them as the dragons swooped down, each one snatching up a sheep.

One of the dragons did not have a good hold of its sheep and dropped it. The sheep fell twenty feet or so to its death. The dragon came back around, landing near his fallen prey, and began to consume it.

The other two dragons had flown out of sight. The knights on the castle walls watched as the large beast devoured its prey. One of the guards grabbed his bow, aimed, and shot an arrow at the dragon, but it landed too short. He tried again, but again the arrow landed too short of its mark.

The bells were still ringing, sending out the warning that dragons were near. Once the dragon had finished his meal, it lifted off the ground and began its flight. The other two had flown off in the direction of the mountain range, but not this one.

Once it was high enough, it headed in the direction of the castle. The knights could see it coming in their direction and prepared to shoot arrows at it. The King had made his way through the courtyard and up the stairs to the castle walls via the cause way. Just as the dragon was over-head, the King saw that the knights were about to release their arrows.

The King cried out, *"Stop... don't shoot!"* but it was too late and one of the knights released his arrow, striking the dragon in its front left leg. The dragon cried out and released a line of fire from its mouth. Flying higher, the dragon turned about and headed down toward the castle in the direction from where the arrow was shot. The King was watching from a distance, the knights were now more scared than disciplined, and they loaded more arrows to shoot at the dragon. This time all four knights on the wall were prepared to release their arrows. The King was not sure what to do, as the knights waited for a command. The King then ordered, *"Loose!"* The four knights re-leased their arrows at the dragon. The dragon veered slightly and all four arrows missed their target this time.

The dragon re-aligned itself and shot a stream of fire at the knights on the castle wall. The dragon was still too high in the sky so the flames from the dragon's mouth did not harm the knights in its path. Turning away from the castle now and heading in the direction of the village, the dragon quickened its speed with many firm flaps of its huge wings.

The King realized where the dragon was headed next. He noticed Sir Lawrence in the courtyard, and called down to him.

"Sir Lawrence, the dragon is headed to the village, take a dozen knights and ride there now. Assist the villagers if they need it." Sir Lawrence turned and began ordering a few knights to the stables to ready the horses.

Thomas and Lady Elizabeth had continued to watch what was transpiring from the moment Thomas first saw the dragons approaching and the warning bells sounded. The window from which they viewed the attack was high enough to watch the entire event unfold. Once the dragons were out of sight, Lady Elizabeth grabbed Thomas by the collar and pulled him along with her out of his room. Heading for her cottage, she had an idea that may hold off the dragons.

The knights that the King sent to the village were arriving, galloping into the village on their horses as they entered the main street. A building at the end of the street was ablaze in fire, people were huddled about looking up at the sky.

The knights hastened their pace down the street toward the burning building. Dismounting their horses, they proceeded to help with putting out the fire.

Sir Lawrence took charge of the situation. The knights' formed a line, a bucket brigade, assisting the small group of villagers already there. The fire had not had a chance to spread to other buildings due to the quick work of the knights and the villagers. No one was hurt, but the villagers were all frightened after witnessing the dragons' attack on the village. It was getting dark now. The villagers were returning to their homes. Sir Lawrence ordered six of his knights to remain behind while he and the others returned to the castle.

CHAPTER 10

"The Threat Is Real"

SIR LAWRENCE APPROACHED the main castle gate with the other knights. Dismounting his horse in the center of the courtyard, he ordered his squire to return his horse to the stables. He walked briskly toward the royal family's residence. He wanted to report to the king as soon as possible the events that transpired in the village.

The King was in the meeting hall hearing testimonials from those who had witnessed the dragons that day.

A farmer was in the middle of his testimony as Sir Lawrence entered the meeting hall.

"Your majesty I was in my field when the dragons flew overhead, heading in the direction of the castle.

There were three of them. Large beasts they were. Their wings spans were huge. All with long tails and scales. I could not believe my eyes!" he exclaimed. "How are you going to protect us from these monsters?" the farmer asked.

The King replied, "We will do what we can. I can dispatch a few knights to your fields, we must insure that the crops are taken care of for the harvest."

The King looked over and saw Sir Lawrence. "What news from the village Sir Lawrence?" Everyone in the room turned to look at Sir Lawrence and waited for his reply.

Sir Lawrence spoke, "One dragon did fly over the village your majesty and set one building on fire. No one was injured. My knights assisted the villagers in putting the fire out and contained it to just the carpenter's shop. However, I'm afraid the shop was totally destroyed."

The King lowered his head for a moment, looked back up at the line of people waiting to give testimony, then spoke, "I will not hear anymore testimonies today. The hour is getting late, *please return to your homes, I must meet with Sir Lawrence."*

The people began mumbling unhappily, they wanted to tell the King what they had come to the meeting room to convey. The King stood up from his chair and headed out of the meeting room with Sir Lawrence. The two of them hurried in the direction of the castle war room.

Six days had passed since the King had dispatched the knights on the expedition to the mountains. Not a single raven had returned to inform the King of their progress. Sir Michael who was leading the expedition had his entire staff accompany him. His squire, stable hand, cook, and a few others. Each of the other nine knights also had their squires and others accompany thcm. Many of the man who traveled with the knights where there to manage the provisions for the journey.

The entire expedition team was close to fifty men. With that many men, the journey was going much slower than if only a few had gone. But it was necessary to send this large a force. It had been generations since an expedition had been sent to the mountain range and new paths would surely need to be blazed. The forest was dense and dark. The legend spoke of evil forces within the dark forest, and even of a mythical castle on the other side of the forest that stood at the base of the mountain peak.

The King and Sir Lawrence went straight to the war table where the model of the castle and surrounding lands were constructed. *"Sir Lawrence, is there any news from the expedition party? Have you heard from Sir Michael?"*

"I am sorry your majesty but I have not. None of the ravens we sent have returned. We have no way of knowing if they delivered your messages," Sir Lawrence replied.

"Keep sending the ravens every day, one will find its way. And send a rider to deliver this message." The King sat down at the table and began to compose a note on parchment. When he finished writing the note, he rolled it up, poured a drop

of hot wax over the edge and pressed the King's seal into the wax.

"At once your majesty," Sir Lawrence replied. He took the parchment from the King's hand, turned and left the war room.

In the morning, it was the beginning of the seventh day of the expedition's journey. Sir Michael had made good progress and the team was closer than they knew to the edge of the forest. What they did not know was what they were about to discover.

Sir Michael was wise and a good leader. He knew his knights well and took advantage of this. He knew who was the strongest and the fastest, and he knew whom he could trust in battle. Part of Sir Michael's strategy to shorten the journey to the mountain range was to send out scouts ahead of the main expedition party to find the fastest route. This strategy had served him well in the past. When morning broke, one of the scouts had returned. He dismounted his horse and approached Sir Michael.

"*My liege, I discovered a clearing only a few miles from here. It appears to be the end of the forest and a clear path to the base of the mountain range. There is a small rise that I could not see over but I am sure that over it is the base of the mountain range. I thought it important to return with this news,*" the scout said.

Sir Michael responded, "*This is good news.*" Everyone was up and breaking camp, waiting for orders on which direction they would be heading that morning. Sir Michael signaled to his squire to bring him his horse. He mounted, and with the scout by his side, ordered "*Lead the way!*" They rode off through the thinning forest in the direction of the clearing. The other knights and squires followed in single file behind them.

It was about noon when they finally came to the clearing that the scout had found. Sir Michael ordered the expedition party to take a break before they were to continue onward.

Sir Michael's second in command was Sir Gregory. A younger knight, Sir Gregory was bright and quick on his feet, good with both sword and bow. As he rode beside Sir Michael, he asked, *"My lord, perhaps we should send out another scout to see what is ahead of us beyond that rise?"*

"Yes, I agree with you Sir Gregory. Distances are deceiving. It appears that the mountain range is just over that next rise but we need to know how far, and what provisions we should gather before we continue. Take five men with you and have one signal back to us from the top of the rise with the green banner once you have a clear view of what lies ahead of us."

Sir Michael sent his squire with Sir Gregory. Sir Gregory then had his squire, the two scouts and one other knight accompany them to ride ahead.

When they reached the top of the hilly rise, Sir Gregory was to raise the green flag and wave it back and forth if it appeared to be safe for the rest of the party to approach. If Sir Gregory did not raise the banner, it would indicate that further investigation was needed before having the rest of the expedition advance.

Sir Michael watched patiently as the scout party approached the top of the rise. They appeared as small figures against the open range with the sun high in the sky above them. Finally they reached the top of the rise. The party stopped, turned back for a moment looking back from where they had come, then turned back again to look forward.

What were they looking at? Why were they not raising a flag to signal the expedition to move forward? A few more moments passed and four of the riders started forward slowly, leaving one rider behind.

Sir Gregory, his squire and two others were amazed at what they had come across. Had they discovered the mystery castle spoken of in the legend? The castle walls were all covered in ivy, and stood twenty feet high. The main gate was closed. There was a drawbridge over the moat, which was down, but the moat surrounding the castle was dry with tall weeds everywhere.

They approached cautiously at first, and then at a slow gallop. Another short ride but not without stress and wonder. The castle was very dark and quiet. No one was manning the walls, no guards were at the gate. There was no sign of any activity.

Sir Michael grew impatient and began to gallop toward the top of the ridge to find out for himself what was going on. When he reached the top, he met up with his squire.

"What is going on?" he bellowed, *"Can we proceed forward?"* Then Sir Michael turned and saw the castle below. His mouth agape, he turned his horse toward the dark castle and without hesitation proceeded to ride toward it.

Meeting up with Sir Gregory, Sir Michael rode across the drawbridge slowly toward the closed front gate. They dismounted their horses. Sir Michael approached the gate on foot with Sir Gregory walking by his side. They both had their hands on their swords, ready to draw them. Together they pushed at the gate, but it did not open.

Sir Gregory walked back to his horse and grabbed a rope. He formed a loop at one end and proceeded to toss it to the top of the gate. The first attempt was successful, catching a pointed pillar at the very top of the wall. Sir Gregory then proceeded to deftly scale the castle wall.

When he reached the top, it was only a few moments before he was able to open the front gate for Sir Michael.

Grabbing the horses reigns, Sir Michael walked forward and entered the castle courtyard. The ground was overgrown with weeds and ivy. It appeared that the castle had been vacant for many years. Everything was covered in dark soot from a fire. Sir Michael's squire and the others entered the castle courtyard a short moment later.

Sir Michael turned to his squire, *"Have the rest of the expedition party advance to the castle, we will set up here, go!"*

Sir Michael's squire remounted his horse and rode off to inform the rest of the knights to advance to the castle.

Sir Michael turned to the two scouts and ordered them to investigate the castle, starting from the top of each wall and the towers. He and Sir Gregory would investigate the main building.

After some time, the scouts found and reported back to Sir Michael, who had settled into a large meeting room inside the main building.

In the front right wall tower the scouts found the ravens' nest. There were fourteen live ravens, each with a message attached to their legs. The expedition had been gone seven days. Each day a raven was sent by Sir Michael to report to the King. Each day the King had sent a raven to the expedition party. The ravens never made it to their destinations, but somehow found their way here to the lost castle's nest, curious!

The scouts removed the messages from their legs and presented them to Sir Michael. Sir Michael ordered his squire to get the court sorcerer, Rhoslyn whom the King had ordered to go with the expedition party. She was a witch and a sorceress, who had been at odds with Lady Elizabeth on many occasions.

Rhoslyn entered the meeting room where Sir Michael was waiting for her, *"You sent for me, my liege?"*

"Yes, tell me what you know of this place, what does the legend say?"

Rhoslyn responded, *"My lord this does appear to be the dark castle the great book talks about. This place was the final battle between the dragons and the kingdom long ago. The dragons practically burned the castle to the ground. The walls are all dark from soot and ash, many knights died defending these castle walls. A great storm blew in from the mountain and the rain was so heavy that it extinguished the fire. The morning after the storm, the great book tells that the dragons were never seen again. After months of searching and waiting for the dragons to return, the castle was abandoned. This is still a mystery to this day. Our ancestors asked, why did the dragons just disappear? The book also explains the prophecy of their return."*

Sir Michael excused Rhoslyn, than sat down at the head of the meeting room table and began to write two notes on parchment. He ordered to have a rider carry one of the notes to the King. The other was to be attached to a raven.

The notes read, *"We have found the lost castle at the foot of the mountain range. We are holding up here and will be sending scouts to the mountains in search of the dragons' lair."*

Sir Michael had a feeling that this raven would find its way to the King.

CHAPTER 11

"Books and Spells"

LADY ELIZABETH FORCED Thomas to go back with her to her cottage. She did not inform the King what she was planning, but she had an idea that she felt she had to investigate.

She remembered reading a passage in one of her books that could give her a deeper clue to the mystery of the prophecy. Now that the dragons had appeared she felt that she needed to do another reading with Thomas. This time alone. Once they reached the cottage, Elizabeth began to search her books. *"Which one was it?"* Frantic to find the right book, she started tossing other books out of the way. The room was soon a total mess as she rummaged through the piles of books.

Then, at last, *"Here it is… this is the one,"* she murmured aloud. Turning the pages, she finally found the passage she remembered. She read it out loud, *"And a boy shall appear from another time, he will look as if to be the twin of the son of royalty. When this comes to pass, the dragons will once again appear in the sky. Only the blue butterfly princess can tame the fury of the dragons."*

Lady Elizabeth turned to Thomas, *"You spoke of seeing a blue butterfly while you were watching your sheep! Is this true?"*

"Yes," Thomas replied. He was standing over by the door studying the carvings on Lady Elizabeth's walking cane. He asked, *"Why are there butterflies and dragons on your staff?"*

"When I was just a little girl I always had the same dream. Dragons and butterflies flying above the fields near the castle. When I grew older, I came across this cottage and the woman who lived here. She was a mystic and sorceress. That staff belonged to her. I started coming here every day and she began to teach me how to read and make potions. Finally

one day I told her about my dream, the dream of the butterflies and dragons. She showed me her staff and the carvings and told me of the prophecy. She said that someday the dragons would return. That time is now."

Elizabeth grabbed her staff from Thomas's hand and moved it to another corner of the room. At that same moment, there was a knock on the door. Elizabeth turned and asked, *"Who's there?"*

"It is Megan!" came the reply. Elizabeth asked, *"Is the prince with you?"*

"No," Megan said as she entered the cottage. Then she continued boldly, *"I want you to teach me how to be a sorceress!"*

"And why would I do that...?" Elizabeth responded puzzled. *"I don't have time for such nonsense, I am too busy! Don't you know what is going on? The prophecy, the dragons have returned and I have to get to the bottom of this and find a way to send them back to where they came from before they burn the kingdom to the ground."*

Megan would not take no for an answer, *"I can read, I can help find whatever it is you are looking for in these books."*

Thomas, wanting to support Megan's request, spoke up, *"The woman who lived here before you helped you and taught you what you know. Aren't two or three heads better than one? I can help too!"*

Elizabeth turned, and saw the mess she had made by tossing all of the books around, looking for that one passage. She sighed and turned back to Megan, *"Fine, you can start by cleaning up this mess and organizing all of these books, oldest to newest. Spell books can go over here, parchment and papers over on that table,"* she ordered. *"Well get started you two!"* she exclaimed with a smile.

Megan and Thomas quickly got started straightening up the cottage. They gathered the books from the floor and made piles. Lady Elizabeth grabbed the book where she found the key passage, left the cottage and headed to the castle to speak with the King.

As Megan and Thomas were sorting the books, one particular book came to their attention. The book was very large, thick and heavy. It had a dark brown cover, bound with two leather straps. A drawing of a dragon was on the front cover flying toward a castle in the distance. Megan unfastened the two leather straps and opened the book. It was very old and the writing was hard to read. Megan turned a few pages and saw more drawings of dragons and the mountains. Thomas looked over her shoulder, reached down and turned to a page in the middle of the book. The drawing showed a castle on fire and three dragons above it breathing white hot flames.

Thomas remarked, *"I think this is the drawing Lady Elizabeth showed the king and the knights in the war room."*

Or was it? Megan studied the drawing closer. *"I'm not so sure!"* she remarked. *"This castle has four towers, one on each corner of the castle walls. Our castle also has four towers, but we have the causeway overlooking the courtyard. There is no causeway in this drawing. See? I think this is a different castle,"* she exclaimed.

Thomas looked down at the drawing more closely, nodding. Megan got up off the floor and carried the book to the nearby table. The two sat down and began looking through the book in more detail, turning more pages, reading what they could make out. Megan's intuition and curiosity began to heighten.

She was beginning to feel like this was truly her calling to become a sorceress just like Lady Elizabeth. She directed Thomas to search through another pile of books and look for anything to do with dragons or castles.

"How about this one? Ancient Castles and Kings," Thomas read the title aloud. *"Or this one. It has a drawing of a butterfly on the cover, Butterfly Potions".* Thomas opened this book and started reading the ingredients of one of the potions.

Enchantment Potion

One butterfly, any size any color
A clump of mud from the silver creek
10 wild berries
A small piece of tree bark from a Maple tree
Mix into a pot of boiling water, stir well
Reduce to one sip
Have subject drink potion at sunset

"I wonder what this potion is for, and what would it do to the person who drinks it?" Thomas wondered aloud.

Megan raised her head and turned to Thomas, *"What are you going on about?"*

"I found this book of Butterfly Potions. Lady Elizabeth was talking about butterflies just before you knocked on the door. Look, see there are butter-fly and dragon carvings on her staff. And the passage in the book she took with her said something about a butterfly princess taming the dragons." Thomas explained.

Megan rushed over to take a look at the staff and then the potion book. *"I think you may have found something here. See if there is a potion that has something to do with dragons."*

Thomas turned the pages quicker now, with Megan looking over his shoulder, looking for a potion with a title of Dragons or something to do with dragons. There was nothing. Not a single potion with the word dragons in the title. The hour was getting late. They had not realized that the sun had set and it was now dark. Thomas looked up and said, *"I'm getting hungry, how about you?"*

Megan nodded in agreement as her stomach growled. *"I wonder when Lady Elizabeth will return. Do you think there is any chance one of these books could be a recipe book?"* Thomas asked chuckling.

Megan replied, *"What's a recipe book?"*

Thomas looked at her incredulously, *"You know, like a cookbook. A book that tells you how to cook food!"*

At that Lady Elizabeth entered the cottage. *"I see you have made some progress! I suppose the two of you expect me to feed you now that it is past supper time."*

"That would be great!" Thomas replied happily. Lady Elizabeth hurriedly began to prepare something for them to eat.

She had not been able to inform the King of her findings from the book as he was out on a hunt when she got to the castle. The guard told her the King was not expected to return until morning.

After dinner, Lady Elizabeth began a second card reading for Thomas. She was hoping to get more insight into his being here and his relationship with the appearance of the dragons in the sky.

She started the reading by checking the position of the planets, sun and moon on the night Thomas was born. Now that she knew his birth date was in the future, she would have to calculate these positions.

"Megan, here is your first lesson. To be a good mystic you must first learn all about the stars and

constellations. You must learn about the position of the sun and moon in these constellations on the day of a person's birth. The lights that we see in the sky every night have much to reveal about who we are and what lay ahead of us as we make our way through life. Come with me, children."

Elizabeth grabbed a shawl from the rack hanging by the door and stepped outside. The three of them walked away from the cottage. Looking up at the sky and the stars shining down, Elizabeth began to explain the twelve constellations that make up the Zodiac. Pointing out the points of light that appeared to be stars, but brighter than the rest, she explained that they were in fact planets. Venus and Saturn were in the sky that night. The moon had not yet risen, which made it easier to see them. Elizabeth showed her how to connect the stars together to make shapes that became constellations.

Thomas was born in November. The constellation Scorpio is the zodiac sign for those born in the month of November. Within the constellation of Scorpio is a cluster of stars. This cluster is known as the Butterfly Cluster which is made up of mostly blue stars.

After going through the Zodiac, Elizabeth led them back to the cottage. She began to look for her book with the drawings of the constellations. She found it in one of the neatly stacked piles of books that Megan had arranged.

She opened the book to the Scorpio constellation and showed Megan and Thomas how the stars made up the scorpion. Then she pointed out the location of the butterfly cluster within the constellation. She got up and motioned for Thomas to join her over at the table where she did her first reading of him.

Thomas whispered to Megan, *"I hope she doesn't want me to drink that disgusting tea again! She makes the worst tea."* Elizabeth was shuffling the deck of cards with the pictures on them. She laid them down on the table as before and asked Thomas to separate the one pile into three piles. He did as she asked. Megan sat down beside Lady

Elizabeth as she believed she was about to get her second lesson.

Lady Elizabeth laid out the cards. The Wheel of Fortune, the Queen of Pentacles and finally the Four of Pentacles. She explained the position of the first card as Thomas's past, the second card was the present and the third card represented the future.

Lady Elizabeth was not surprised that the first card was the Wheel of Fortune. The picture on the card showed a wheel with the symbols of each Zodiac constellation appearing around it. Clearly it was fate and destiny that brought Thomas to this time. The wheel represented chance and change. The card in the middle position, the Queen of Pentacles, represented the present moment. Lady Elizabeth saw herself in this card. The queen of Pentacles is confident and hard working. The queen is often successful in all of her pursuits. From this card, Lady Elizabeth grows more confident that she will find the answer she seeks to rid the kingdom of the dragons.

The four of Pentacles appeared in the third position, the future. The card depicts a merchant holding tightly on to four pentacles, the rewards of his hard work. The fear of loss needs to be overcome to see the true success of winning the battle.

Lady Elizabeth saw the outcome of the reading to be positive and explained it to Megan and Thomas the best she could. *"The cards have revealed the truth. I will find the answers we seek, and you Thomas, must be returned to your own time."*

CHAPTER 12
"The Hunt"

THE KING, PRINCE Samuel and a few others had gone off on a hunt. Hunting was a part of everyday life. Even with the threat of dragons attacking the castle, it was necessary to complete the normal tasks of everyday living. This hunt would be short. They would be out for just one day and one night in the forest, looking for small game, rabbit, deer or perhaps wild turkey. The hunting party had made their preparations the night before and in the early morning they would make their way to the forest. Once in the trees, they would look for a clearing to make a small campsite before setting out on foot to look for prey. They hunted using bows and arrows. A lot of practice was needed to learn to be a good shot, especially for small game. The Prince had been getting better over the past few months hitting stationary targets, but hitting a moving target like a rabbit was another thing entirely.

King James and Samuel paired up and started their walk into the deep woods. The King's squire and another junior knight paired and followed behind them. A few others remained behind at the campsite.

Hunting requires patience. It involves a lot of walking and waiting in silence. After a few hours, Samuel was getting tired and asked his father if they could rest. The King agreed. He knew the forest well and suggested they go to a nearby stream. As they walked toward the stream, Samuel heard movement off to his left. He turned and saw a small doe feeding on a bush close by. The King was already aware of the doe. He had drawn his bow, his arrow ready to be released. Samuel was staring at the doe and walked right in front of his father. Samuel was unaware that he had stepped in front of him and now pointing at him. To get the King's attention, Samuel hissed, *"Father!"*

The deer jerked its head towards them and immediately ran off. An opportunity wasted. The King bellowed, *"Son, you know better!"* He shook his head and continued, *"Well at least we know we are in the right area now. Where there is one there will be others. Let's continue on to the stream and get some fresh water. We will hunt again after a short break. There are still a few more hours of daylight before we need to head back to the camp."*

The stream was not far, and as they got closer you could hear the water rushing over the small waterfall. The King handed Samuel his waterskin and had him fill it with fresh water. Samuel sat on a large rock at the edge of the stream and held the waterskin to the water's surface. The King began to tell Samuel of one of his hunting outings with his father.

"Son, I sat on that very same rock where you are now the first time my father took me on a hunt. I was filling my waterskin the same way you are right now. The next thing I knew, I was in the water

floating downstream toward that waterfall. I could not swim. I was screaming and slashing about, and I could see my father running along the side of the stream trying to find a way to get to me. He was yelling to me, telling me to grab on to something, anything," the King's gaze wandered down the stream toward the waterfall as he spoke.

"I was able to grab a branch that was hanging down from a fallen tree just a hundred feet from the drop. Your grandfather was then able to reach me and he pulled me out. I will never forget how cold that water was, it went right through me it did. Made me feel like I would never be warm again," the King shuddered.

Samuel was looking behind the King's shoulder as he told the story. He started pointing in the direction behind the King, trying desperately to get his father's attention. Finally, the King realized and turned. He saw a twelve point buck staring back at the two of them. Slowly, they got to their feet collected their bows. The King gestured to Samuel to go to the right, while he circled around to the left, toward the buck. The buck was moving slowly away from them, but had not sensed the threat. Even so, it had its eyes on the King. Samuel was now behind the buck while the king remained in its line of sight. Samuel was in a position to shoot. He raised his bow, pulled back his arrow, and without hesitation, released. The arrow struck the buck in the neck, just as it had turned its head back towards Samuel.

Samuel had just made his first kill. The King ran to the buck as did Samuel. *"Son, you got him! This will be cause for a feast! We will celebrate back at the castle tomorrow. Great shot, I could not have done better myself,"* the King said smiling broadly.

Meanwhile, Megan and Thomas had spent the night at Lady Elizabeth's cottage. Eleanor was furious that Megan had not come home. She assumed that she was with Lady Elizabeth and headed out to find her once her work was done for the Queen. When Eleanor arrived at the cottage, she knocked on the door forcefully. Megan opened the door to see her mother standing there, and immediately began apologizing for not returning home to the castle.

"What is the meaning of this?" Eleanor interrupted Megan furiously. *"I was so worried about you! You run off, don't tell me where you are going and I find you here, just as I suspected."* Lady Elizabeth was looking at Eleanor as she lectured her daughter, with Thomas next to her.

Eleanor turned to Lady Elizabeth, *"And you, what is this nonsense you are putting into her head?"* She grabbed a book from Megan's hand. Then she turned again to speak to the boy but realized she was not sure who she was seeing. *Was this the prince or the boy Megan told her about who looks like the prince?*

"Your majesty…" she started courteously, but Thomas quickly replied, *"I'm Thomas, I'm not the prince."*

Eleanor nodded curtly and then turned back to Megan, *"Get your things, you're coming back with me."* Megan went over to the table where she had left her bag, she quickly snuck two books inside.

Eleanor stepped toward her wanting her to hurry up. She grabbed her by the arm and pulled her out the door and they headed back to the castle.

The expedition party had not made any progress on locating the dragons' lair. They had settled into the dark castle and made it as comfortable as possible in the short time since they had arrived there.

Then all of sudden the next day, three dragons appeared in the sky above the dark castle. The guard in the north tower began ringing the warning bell. Flying in a 'V' formation like geese, one dragon led the other two. Sir Michael, Sir Gregory and the mystic Rhoslyn all hurried out of the meeting room to see what was happening. From the castle courtyard they saw the dragons in the sky, high above the castle, flying in the direction of the village.

"Send a raven at once!" Sir Michael yelled up to the guard on the north tower. The dragons flew swiftly, it would not take them long to reach the village. *Could the raven get to the castle before them?* Sir Michael was not sure of this. Within

a few moments, the raven with its message was released from the ravens' nest and flew in the direction the dragons had gone. Sir Michael, Sir Gregory and Rhoslyn returned to the meeting room to continue to discuss where the lair could possibly be.

Rhoslyn had found a passage in one of her ancient books, which spoke of the dragons' lair. The passage read;

"Look to the highest point to find the lair, but you will find the dragons not. Now look below and there you will find what you seek.

Beware the trap to lore you in, else there you will stay forever more, for the dragons can see from whence you came."

Going outside again, the three of them went to the north tower to get a better look of the mountain range, searching for the highest peak.

"There my lord," Sir Gregory pointed. *"The highest peak. And just below it, an outcropping of*

rock, surely a cave!" Rhoslyn looked at her book and a sketch of the mountain range, *"Yes my lord, it is here in the book."*

Sir Michael turned to look at the book and then back to the mountains. *"We have no time to waste, the dragons are gone from their lair. We must get to that peak and prepare for their return. It is then that we can catch them by surprise."* Hurrying down from the north tower, Sir Michael ordered his squire to make preparations to head up the mountain within the hour.

King James, Samuel and the hunting party were returning to the castle. Samuel's buck, a few rabbits and a couple wild turkeys were all loaded onto the wagon. The guards at the castle gate greeted them. One of them announced the return of the King, shouting, *"Open the gate, the King has returned! Open the gate!"* Those milling about in the courtyard turned to the front gate. All were happy to see that the hunt had been successful.

Samuel was very proud of his buck and hoped that Megan would be there to greet him, but there was no sign of her as the hunting party entered the courtyard. Sir Lawrence came out from the great meeting room, as well as those there to discuss needs or complaints. A small crowd began to gather to greet the return of the King, but mostly to fuss over the twelve point buck.

When the Queen came out to meet them, the King explained to Katherine how Samuel shot the buck, and that they should prepare for a feast. *"This is a proud day for our young prince! Kass, with one arrow he brought down this buck, right through the neck, a twelve pointer! A feast I say, let's have a feast to celebrate the hunt."* King James exclaimed proudly. He grabbed his son's hand and raised his arm high into the air to the happy shouts and applause from the crowd.

There was a lot of buzz in the courtyard. Some of Samuel's sparring partners, sons of some of the knights, came out to see what the commotion was about. Samuel ran over to tell them how he had killed the buck. As he began to explain, Megan and Eleanor entered the courtyard. The Queen saw Eleanor and called her over. The Queen ordered her to immediately start preparing for a feast for the return of the hunting party. This left Megan alone for a moment and she wandered over to see Samuel.

Samuel turned and saw her, but was still disappointed that she was not there when he first arrived. He turned back to the group and continued his story. As Megan approached, one of the knight's sons turned and spoke to her in a demeaning tone, *"What do you want peasant? Your prince is busy telling us of his conquest, don't you have some bedpans to clean?"* Megan did not speak. Her head lowered, she turned and walked away, hurt that Samuel had not acknowledged her or come to her defense.

Samuel heard what had been said, but continued with his story of how he had snuck up on the buck and killed it with just one arrow.

The next day was extremely busy for everyone; preparing for a feast was a lot of hard work. Decorating the great meeting hall and preparing the food were only parts of what needed to be done. The minstrels, bards and other royal entertainers had to be notified. The wives of all of the knights were frantic with putting together ensembles that would make them stand out at the feast.

CHAPTER 13

"The Dragons Return"

THINGS WERE COMING together as always when a royal feast was planned. The scribes were dispatched to the village to notify the villagers of the great feast to celebrate the hunt. The minstrels, jugglers, and acrobats began arriving at the castle by noon. The great meeting hall was decorated with ribbons, flags and flowers. The tables had been rearranged to accommodate as many people as possible. Everything was in order and the festivities would begin by midafternoon.

Eleanor was helping the Queen dress while Megan was being punished and told to stay in her chambers. The day's open meetings with the King in the great meeting room were cancelled since the hall would be used for the feast. The village merchants used events like this to sell their goods and were allowed to set up areas in the castle courtyard. They too were the first to arrive at the castle with their carts and wagons loaded with wares to sell. Fabric, leather goods, dresses, jewelry, pottery, tools, swords, baked goods and even live animals like chickens, rabbits and squirrels. It was not long before the courtyard was filled with merchants setting up their stalls as the villagers began to arrive for the feast.

The King had a special surprise arranged for Samuel. He was having the antlers from the buck mounted for Samuel to hang in his room. Once the Queen was ready, all of the members of the royal court would proceed from the royal chambers through the castle courtyard. Just below the causeway that overlooks the courtyard, a small stage was set up. The royal procession would end there. The King would address all who were present and formally start the feast.

The Queen was ready and Eleanor went to in-

form the royal trumpeters to sound the announce-
ment that the procession was about to begin. The
members of the royal court lined up as the trumpeters began to play. Everyone in the courtyard
stopped and turned their attention to the royals
as the procession began. Queen Katherine was
dressed in a gray and maroon gown with lace em-
broidery. The silver and gold crown on her head
glittered as she was escorted by King James. The
King wore leather attire trimmed with royal blue
fabric and white fox tail fur.

There were some members of the royal court
missing as they were still on the expedition, but
those who were there were dressed in their best
clothes. The royal physician and his wife, the
chancellor and his wife and the grand master
of the hunt were also present. The grand master
would be presenting the mounted twelve point
antlers to the prince.

The trumpeters played until the procession
reached the stage. Everyone quieted and the
King stood at the front of the stage to address the

crowd. *"My good people, we are here today to celebrate the hunt. My son, your prince, has provided us with the prize of a twelve point buck which we will feast on this day."*

The master of the hunt rose from his station, uncovered the mounted antlers and presented them to Prince Samuel.

The sound of the tower bells began to ring, but not in celebration of the hunt. Three dragons were approaching from the north, flying directly toward the castle. Those on the ground were cheering, thinking this was all part of the celebration. The bells began sounding louder and were tolling for longer than expected. The King looked up and saw the dragons approaching the north castle wall. Sir Lawrence was at the King's side and followed his gaze to the sky. *"My Lord!"*

Sir Lawrence shouted to the crowd; *"Take cover! Hurry, take cover!"* One dragon swooped down to where they were roasting the twelve point buck on a large spit over the open fire pit. The cooks ran for cover and cleared the area as the dragon landed and began tearing at the buck. Another dragon soon landed next to it. Sharing the buck, both were now devouring it.

The people were running everywhere, screaming in a panic. Sir Lawrence jumped from the stage to organize his knights to action and protect the people. Two of the knights on the wall drew their bows and released arrows at the one dragon still flying above the castle. The arrows missed as the dragon quickly changed direction to avoid them. Then it turned back toward the knights on the wall and released a stream of fire from its mouth. Both men ducked and ran to the bell tower for cover, unharmed.

Megan, who had been restricted to her room, heard all of the commotion outside and ran to the window. Looking down, she saw the panic of the people in the courtyard and the two dragons feasting on the buck. Looking up she saw one dragon flying in the sky. It was now headed toward the large tree on the west side of the castle. But something else as well, a person walking toward the tree. *Who is that?* Megan noticed that the person was walking with a staff. It could only be one person. Lady Elizabeth.

She had to warn Lady Elizabeth. Megan jerked around and quickly grabbed her bag. In it were the last two books she had been reading when her mother found her in the cottage. When her mother had asked her to get her things, she had snuck these two books into her bag before leaving.

While Megan was hurrying to the castle doors, the dragon had changed its direction in the sky once more. It returned to the castle, landing in the courtyard with the other dragons and started toward the buck. When the third and largest of the three dragons landed, the other two dragons took to the sky. Flying above, they breathed jets of fire down at the peasants, merchants and knights while the largest dragon feasted on the buck alone.

Many of the merchant carts and wagons were ablaze. The knights began forming bucket brigades to put out the fires and keep them from spreading to the castle walls and buildings. Chaos was all around, people were running everywhere.

After the buck had been picked clean by the dragon, he took to the sky again. It was breathing more flames in the direction of the castle, and a line of knights was poised to fire arrows at the beast. As the flames came too close, they were forced to duck and the knights' arrows missed their mark. The largest dragon was once again flying in the direction of the tree on the west side of the castle. Megan was now only a hundred yards from Lady Elizabeth and she called out, but Elizabeth did not hear her. Lady Elizabeth was too focused on her mission. She had found another passage in the book of butterflies. She was determined to catch a blue butterfly, as the book indicated that this was a key to sending Thomas back to his own time. Just by chance Lady Elizabeth had spotted a blue butterfly and was making her way to catch it in her net. Sneaking up to it, she waved her net and with one swift motion the butterfly was caught.

Megan was now only a hundred feet from Lady Elizabeth, she called out to her again. *"Lady Elizabeth! The dragons! The dragons are back!"* Elizabeth turned and saw Megan, but just then a dragon swooped down out of the sky right behind her. Elizabeth yelled terrified, *"Look out!"* Megan turned and dropped to the ground, but the dragon grabbed her with his large talons and lifted her into the air as his powerful wings pushed hard to gain more altitude.

Screaming with terror, Megan looked down, seeing the ground getting farther and farther away as the dragon powered its way higher into the sky. The dragon let out a huge roar and then another. The other two dragons attacking the castle withdrew from their attack and flew to join the lead dragon carrying Megan.

Lady Elizabeth stood in disbelief and knew there was nothing she could do. She rushed to the castle to inform the King of what had happened. The new passages she had found in the ancient book of butterflies, the connection with Thomas, and now the capture of Megan by the dragon.

Back at the castle the situation was beginning to calm down. It appeared that no one had been hurt directly by the dragons. Some received injuries from the fires and the chaos of people running for cover. As Lady Elizabeth entered the courtyard, she found King James standing with Sir Lawrence. Queen Katherine, the prince and Thomas were only a few feet away, also assessing the damage brought on by the dragons' attack.

"Your majesty," Lady Elizabeth spoke urgently as she approached them, *"I found several ancient passages in one of my books that may help us."* The blue butterfly was still captured in her net, and it started to fly about in the little space it had available. Thomas noticed it and rushed over to Lady Elizabeth. *"You caught one, you caught a blue butterfly! I told you it was real, I told you all..."* he trailed off. The King and Sir Lawrence looked

at the net and saw the blue butterfly inside. Sir Lawrence asked, *"What of this passage? What does this have to do with butterflies and the boy? Surely a butterfly has no power over a dragon!"*

"My lord, in order to return the boy to his own time, we need the butterfly and the potion I have prepared. The moon will be full in ten days. We must take the boy to the tree with the blue butterfly and cast them into the tree's opening on the night of the full moon."

"And what will this do?" the king asked. Elizabeth replied, *"The boy will be returned to his own time and the dragons will no longer plunder the kingdom."*

"And this is what it says in your books?" the King asked in a doubtful tone. *"I don't have faith in your books and passages. The expedition has located the dragons' lair. I will ride to the dark castle tonight with more knights and we will kill the dragons just as my great, great, great grandfather did before me and the kingdom will once again be free from threats from the sky."*

As the King finished speaking, Eleanor ran over in a panic, *"Has anyone seen Megan!? She is not in her room!"* Lady Elizabeth replied calmly, *"She's been taken by the dragon."*

Eleanor stared at her aghast, *"How is this possible, this cannot be true!?"* Eleanor was very upset by the possibility. *"I'm sorry, but I was there when the dragon snatched her. I was collecting the blue butterfly by the great tree and the dragon swooped down and took her,"* Lady Elizabeth explained.

Samuel and Thomas turned to look at each other. They were concerned by the abduction of their friend and what would happen to her. *"Father we must go and rescue her,"* Samuel said, not thinking of how this would sound. His true feelings for Megan, a peasant girl, were being revealed to the King. The King turned to Samuel and saw in his eyes that he truly cared for the girl.

The King nodded and turned to Sir Lawrence. *"Make preparations for our journey to the dark castle, we leave at first light. Take Thomas and have two guards watch him, have them do as Lady*

Elizabeth instructs." "Father, I want to come with you!" cried Samuel.

"No son, you must remain here at the castle. In times of war, there must always be an heir to the throne here at the castle." The King turned and walked away swiftly with Sir Lawrence.

CHAPTER 14

"Return of the Dragon Princess"

MEGAN HAD PASSED out from fear, but after a few minutes she awoke. The dragons were flying in the direction of the mountain range. Below she could see the river winding across the countryside. A voice in her head was telling her to remain calm, but then the dragon went into a steep dive toward the ground. Megan began screaming, fearing the dragon would drop her. After what seemed like ages the dragon slowed his descent and landed near the river. Releasing her from his talons, she stood and slowly stepped away. She knew it would make no sense to run and instead she stood just ten feet from the large beast.

The other two dragons followed down from the sky, landing nearby. Both walked over to the river to take a drink of water, but it was more like huge gulps. The larger dragon, the one that had carried her, approached the river. He dipped his head into the water, pulled up a fish and swallowed it whole. The dragon then turned and looked straight at Megan, she was still standing there just ten feet from him. The same voice inside her head, not her own, spoke to her, *"We have longed for your return, the journey is not much farther, just a short flight over that first set of mountains."*

Megan was puzzled by this voice in her head, it sounded like nothing she had ever heard before. *"You speak?"* she murmured aloud. The dragon still stared at her and replied, but again she only heard it in her head.

"I am ORMR. That is Mindy and her twin sister Melinda," he said, turning his head in their direction as they continued to drink from the river. *"Not big on fish, those two. They prefer a nice*

lamb to feast on, a deer or a human..." The dragon seemed to smile at this last remark.

"What do you want with me? Are you going to eat me?" Megan asked bravely. *"We have been asleep for several hundred years. When we awoke, we sensed your presence. We must be on our way though, we need your magic to awaken the nest before the coming full moon."*

ORMR approached Megan to grab her, but she backed away afraid. *"Do you remember how to ride?"* ORMR asked. Megan shook her head no. *"Just climb on my back and hold on tight."*

Megan approached ORMR, stepped up on his knee and climbed on to his back at the base of his neck. *"Hold on!"* said the voice in her head. Just as she was getting settled on the dragon's back, she jerked back, almost falling off. A few powerful strokes from his mighty wings and ORMR was in the air. Mindy and Melinda followed after a moment.

Fresh snow had fallen at the very top of the mountain the night before. Sir Gregory and his team had managed to make their way to the dragons' lair and surprisingly they had found it without difficulty. Fearful of the passage that Rhoslyn had found in the ancient book, they approached cautiously.

The passage had said,

"Look to the highest point to find the lair,
but you will find the dragons not. Now look
below and there you will find what you seek.
Beware the trap to lore you in, else there you
will stay forever more, for the dragons can see
from whence you came."

Sir Gregory drew his sword and told the others to keep a sharp eye as he approached the opening. He looked above to the peaks, taking note of how much snow had fallen that night. He could feel the wind blowing, just enough to give him a chill as he approached the entrance of the cave. He entered the lair, and had only gone a few steps when he noticed a broken shield on the ground to his left.

A few feet farther laid a knight's helmet. The farther into the cave he went, the darker it got, making it hard to see. It took a few moments before Sir Gregory's eyes adjusted to the darkness of the lair.

He walked slowly, deeper and deeper, when he stumbled over something and fell to the ground, dropping his sword. Reaching to pick up his sword, his fingers clasped around something that was not his sword. He dropped it quickly, realizing what it was. *Bone.* Everywhere around him, bones. *Were they human? Animal?* He was not sure, it was too dark to determine.

He stood up quickly, his hand now had a much tighter grip on the sword handle. He moved away from where he had fallen, and to his right he noticed a group of what appeared to be rocks, but they had a familiar shape. *Eggs ... Dragon eggs ...* He knew he had seen enough and headed back out of the cave, this was surely the dragon's lair.

Sir Gregory made his way back to the others who were anxiously waiting for him.

"It's a death trap. There is no way we can fight the dragons from inside the lair. But I have an idea…" he said as he looked up at the freshly fallen snow above the cave entrance.

"Once the dragons are inside, we need to find a way to get the snow to cover the opening. Then the dragons will be trapped inside."

Lady Elizabeth was still researching the ancient books and trying to decipher the meaning of the passages she had found. The King was already making his way to the dark castle with a small group, which included his squire and two others.

ORMR, Mindy and Melinda were getting close to their lair as they flew high in the sky. As the mountain peak came into view, they started their decent. Megan felt more comfortable on ORMR's back but as he started his descent, she slipped off his back, screaming as she fell. ORMR quickly reacted and flew down to catch her with his great claws.

"I think I better carry you the rest of the way," the voice in Megan's head said. Megan did not

respond as she had once again passed out from the fear of the fall.

The dragons approached their lair from the air. Mindy and Melinda arrived first, landing just in front of the entrance followed by ORMR. Sir Gregory and his team had climbed above the cave opening, almost to the top of the mountain.

Hiding behind a large bolder they saw the dragons approach. *"The big one is carrying something, or someone!"* Sir Gregory remarked to the others. ORMR landed and laid Megan on the ground, releasing her from his claws. She remained motionless, still unconscious. ORMR began nudging her with his snout.

Christopher, Sir Gregory's squire, raised his bow and prepared to release his arrow. Sir Gregory signaled to him to hold.

After a few nudges, Megan came to and stood up, brushing herself off. Megan turned and walked toward the cave entrance, checking that she still had her bag with her. ORMR came up behind her and they entered the cave.

Sir Gregory's plans were about to change. He could not trap the dragons inside knowing that a person would be trapped along with them. *Whoever they have taken will surely become the dragon's next meal,* he thought. He would have to come up with a way to rescue them before causing the avalanche that would trap the dragons.

Mindy and Melinda had already made it down to their nest and had lit the cave by shooting flames of fire at naturally made torches on the walls.

Megan was not aware that Mindy and Melinda were sitting on eggs, providing them the needed warmth to hatch. As Megan looked for a place to sit, she noticed something hanging from the rock wall to her left. She approached it, and saw what appeared to be a large set of blue wings.

As she got closer she realized that it was a costume, a butterfly costume. A thought came to her as she sat down on a rock and opened her bag quickly. Inside were the two books she had taken from Lady Elizabeth's cottage;

Butterfly Potions and Dragon Magic.

By chance she opened the *Butterfly Potions* book to the exact page of a drawing of the butterfly costume. Looking up at the costume on the wall, she was amazed to realize that this was the same exact costume as the one on the page. Megan read the words on the page next to the drawing,

"Only the true Dragon Princess can wield the power from the blue butterfly's armor."

ORMR noticed that she had found the blue butterfly armor. *"What are you waiting for? You will need your wings to fly with us. Only you can get to the pollen from the Goldenrod flower. We need the pollen from the flower for the dragon eggs to hatch. We will rest tonight and set out at first light in the morning for the pollen."*

Megan reached up to take the beautiful butterfly wings down from the wall. She was shaking a little and hesitated for a moment before putting on the wings. At first, nothing seemed to be happening, but then a blue light started to shine around her. The wings began to illuminate and a tingling sensation ran through her body. What was just a costume hardened into a suit of armor around her frame. The wings firmed and with a slight flutter, she was lifted into the air a foot from the ground beneath her. *"I'm fly-flying..."* she stammered, *"I'm flying!"*

"Your majesty," ORMR spoke. This time Megan heard his words not in her head, but with her ears. Mindy and Melinda lifted their heads from their nest and looked over at Megan. Mindy turned to Melinda, *"I told you she was the one, I knew it all along..."*

"You did not, you never believed it!" Melinda remarked. Megan was hearing them speak for the first time. The two of them continued to bicker back and forth for a few minutes.

ORMR shook his head and sighed, then turned to Megan, *"You need your rest. At first light we fly to the cliffs on the other side of the mountain.*

CHAPTER 15

The Dragon's Lair

THE GUARDS WATCHING over Thomas had taken him to the dungeon. It was dark and cold and they had locked him in one of the rooms. There was only a stool to sit on, a bucket and a mound of hay for a bed. The guards had their own ideas about Thomas and saw him as a sorcerer. They had heard stories that he could cast spells and turn a person to stone. They believed that he had cast a spell on the prince and the royal family which caused them to take a liking to him. They thought he was the reason the dragons had returned and they were very afraid. They would be happy to see him go and they waited for Lady Elizabeth's instructions.

The days went by slowly for some, but faster for others. The King rode hard and long each day to get to the dark castle.

Samuel, with the guidance of his mother and Sir Lawrence, took on the role of the King in his father's absence. He sat each day on the throne for the daily meeting in the great hall for the villagers. He listened to their complaints, needs and fears.

Sir Gregory and his team were working to find a way to cause an avalanche that would trap the dragons in their cave.

Lady Elizabeth was still researching her books, looking for anything she had missed. The key she would need to send Thomas back to his own time. She had the blue butterfly, but there was something else she needed. She remembered reading about it in one of her books but could not remember which one.

She looked everywhere in her cottage for it and could not find it. As she searched, she was hoping that when she saw the cover it would reminder her what it was she needed to help Thomas.

She sat down at her table, her crystal ball and wand in hand. The table was lit with a half dozen candles. The cottage was dark except for the light from the candles. Elizabeth was waving her wand over the crystal ball and repeating her mantra. *"Show me the book I seek, Show me the book.... Where is the book I seek, Where is the book I seek?"* she continued to chant, constantly waving the wand. The crystal ball was cloudy inside and nothing was happening. Then, there was an image, an image in the crystal. A face appeared, Eleanor, the queen's chambermaid. She knocked on the door of the cottage, Megan answered it, then Megan moving toward this very table. There were two books on the table, then they were gone. Lady Elizabeth realized now that Megan had taken the book she so desperately needed. The book of butterfly potions.

After many days and nights, the King finally had the dark castle in sight. From the top of the ridge, his squire Paul was pointing down to the dark castle from his horse. *"Your majesty, the cas-*

tle is very close!" Then, as he looked just beyond the castle to the mountain range, he exclaimed, *"Look! There in the distance, a dragon!"* The King and the others followed his gaze and saw the dragon off in the distance. The King nudged his horse forward and called out. His horse jerked him back in his saddle as it lurched forward toward the castle in a gallop. The others followed close behind.

When they arrived at the castle gate, the guard announced their coming, *"Open the gate! The King! Open the gate for the King!"* The guard at the bottom of the gate complied and opened the gate as the King and the three others rode into the courtyard. Sir Gregory came out of the meeting room to greet him. *"Your majesty, we received your raven, we have been expecting you. We have located the dragons' lair and believe we have a way to trap them inside. My knights are making the preparations, but it appears that the dragons have captured someone. They took someone into the cave with them when they first arrived a few days ago."*

The King walked with Sir Gregory into the meeting room as he continued to inform him of the situation.

"Yes, I'm aware of who the dragons took. She is the daughter of the Queen's chambermaid. Is she alive?" Sir Gregory replied *"Yes, but we cannot say for how much longer."* King James turned to him in earnest, *"Is there a way to get her away from the dragons before any harm comes to her?"*

"I'm not sure your majesty. I have been to the dragon's lair. There was only one way in and one way out that we could find. It's a death trap for anyone who enters." Sir Gregory had brought back the knight's helmet that he found in the cave just inside the entrance. It was sitting on the table in the meeting room. King James took notice of it and picked it up. He was studying the markings and asked, *"Where did you find this?"*

"At the entrance to the cave of the dragon's lair." The helmet had the royal family's crest cast into the left side. The helmet was singed and scorched from fire, perhaps from a dragon's flame.

Rhoslyn entered the room as King James continued to study the scorched helmet. *"That is your great, great, great grandfather's helmet. My lord I was not sure at first, but I found a drawing of it here in this book."* King James turned to look at the page she was indicating. *"That is the very same helmet he wore when he slayed his dragon. Many knights died during that quest, leaving the castle in ruins."* A worried look came over the King's face as he placed the helmet back on the table. *"What is our course of action Sir Gregory?"*

"We will have to sneak into the cave at night to rescue the girl. Once she is safe we can trap the dragons inside with an avalanche. With winter coming the dragons will be trapped inside with no food or water. They will surely die of starvation before the summer thaw." The king was nodding his head in approval for this plan. *"We saw one of the dragons flying to the west as we approached the castle. Do we know where the other two dragons are?"*

"Yes my lord, we believe they are in the dragon's lair. When the other one returns, we should sneak

into the cave and rescue the girl. We have been watching the cave entrance. It appears that once each day the largest dragon flies off, carrying something on its back, then it returns at sundown."

"We will rest tonight and tomorrow we will make our attempt to rescue Megan," The King replied.

The next morning the King and the others were up early. The King went to the north tower to watch for the dragon to leave the lair. Just as Sir Gregory had said, the largest dragon appeared with something on its back and headed to the cliffs on the other side of the mountain range, away from the dark castle.

Megan was riding ORMR's back and was wearing her blue butterfly armor. Once ORMR and Megan arrived at the cliffs, Megan released her grip on ORMR's neck and with her wings, flew down to the patch of Goldenrod flowers to collect their pollen. Sir Gregory, the King and a few other knights had begun their hike up to the cave to get into position for the night's mission to rescue Megan and trap the dragons inside the cave.

Lady Elizabeth only had one way to contact the King to let him know what she needed, a raven. She had written a note and had the raven keeper send the message. The message instructed the King to get the book *Butterfly Potions* from Megan. She knew that Rhoslyn would know which potion she would need. Once Rhoslyn had the book she could copy the potion and then send it back to her by raven. Once Lady Elizabeth had the potion she could send Thomas back.

ORMR and Megan returned to the lair at sunset. The King and Sir Gregory were in position and observed their return. ORMR landed in front of the cave entrance. *"What is that on the dragon's back?"* the King asked. *"We cannot say for sure your majesty,"* replied Sir Gregory, *"We cannot get close enough to see without being discovered."* Megan loosened her grip on ORMR's neck and flew into the cave on her own. *"It looks like a giant blue butterfly!"* the King remarked, puzzled. The men stared at the butterfly wonderingly.

Megan went deep into the dragon's lair to deliver the pollen she had collected for the dragon eggs. Mindy and Melinda moved off of their eggs so Megan could cover them with the yellow dust. Afterwards, Megan and the dragons went to sleep.

The King and Sir Gregory approached the cave and entered the dragon's lair. They moved in very slowly and quietly. The cave had some light from a few torches stuck into the cave walls. One of the torches was near Megan's butterfly armor that was hanging on the wall just above where Megan was sleeping.

The King crept up to her and covered her mouth in case she made a noise. He shook Megan to wake her. She awoke suddenly and afraid, unsure what was happening. *"Megan, we are here to rescue you,"* the King whispered, *"Stay quiet, we do not want to wake the dragons."* Next to Megan was her bag containing the two books she had taken from Lady Elizabeth's cottage. The King noticed the bag and took a quick look inside to see if the books were there. Sir Gregory was standing off to the side keeping an eye on the dragons as they slept. He signaled to the King to hurry as Mindy stirred in her sleep. The King grabbed her bag as they stood up. King James and Sir Gregory were getting anxious now, fearing they were taking too long to get out of the cave. As they snuck past ORMR, his head was turned away from them, but then he stirred and turned his head toward them. His eyes were closed though, he was still asleep.

Even so, all three froze in their tracks. They stood absolutely still for a few seconds, holding their breath and trying not to make a sound. ORMR did not move again so they quickened their pace and moved closer to the cave opening.

"My wings...," Megan said as they approached the cave's entrance. Sir Gregory grabbed her arm and whispered menacingly to her, *"Quiet, you will wake the dragons!"* He pulled her along now, trying to navigate the rocky terrain in the dark. They proceeded down the mountain to the first

line of trees. *"I think we can rest for a moment,"* King James said. He again looked into the bag to ensure the books where still inside. Megan addressed the King boldly, *"Your majesty we have to go back for my wings. I need my wings."*

"What are you going on about girl?" Megan replied, *"I need my wings to collect the pollen for the dragon eggs. The dragons need my help your majesty."* Sir Gregory was listening as she spoke. *"You are helping the dragons?"* He said incredulously. *"Your majesty I need to give the signal."* Once they were at a safe distance from the cave, the signal to the knights was a flaming arrow. When the knights saw the arrow, they would cause the avalanche to trap the dragons inside. King James turned to Sir Gregory, *"Give the signal."* With that, Sir Gregory took an arrow from his quiver, loaded it onto his bow and lit the point. Then he aimed high into the sky and released it.

The arrow shot off into the night sky like a falling star. It was clearly visible to anyone who was watching for it. The knights saw the flaming arrow and prepared to start the avalanche. The knights had dragged several tree logs above the cave entrance. They pushed the logs along with half a dozen boulders and forced them to roll down the mountainside. As the logs and boulders starting crashing down the mountain, the freshly fallen snow also started to thunder down toward the cave opening.

Louder and louder, the sound of the avalanche began to echo in the valley, causing more snow to slide down the hills. It was working, the debris was covering the opening to the dragons' lair. The mission had been a success and the dragons were now trapped. Megan was staring up in horror at the entrance to the cave, while the King and Sir Gregory smiled to see that the plan had worked.

CHAPTER 16
"Was It Just A Dream?"

In The Morning, King James, Sir Gregory and the others returned to the dark castle. From the north wall it was clear to see that the cave had been completely covered by the avalanche. King James had given the books from Megan's bag to Rhoslyn. She was hurriedly paging through *Butterfly Potions*, looking for the last ingredient Lady Elizabeth would need to send Thomas back to his time. At last she found it, the Blue Butterfly potion.

Pollen from the Yellow Goldenrod Flower
One blue butterfly
Bark from the great tree
Rain from a storm
A strike of lightning

Rhoslyn copied the potion onto a piece of parchment and tied it to the raven's leg. The raven flew off immediately to Lady Elizabeth's cottage. The expedition party began to make their preparations to return to the kingdom.

The King asked for a few volunteers to remain behind a few days to ensure the dragons were trapped. Everyone was standing in the castle courtyard when the guard on the north tower began sounding the bell. Everyone looked up to the sky. The dragons were approaching fast. Somehow they had managed to find their way out. Everyone started hurrying about, running for their defensive positions on the castle walls.

ORMR was leading Mindy and Melinda as they approached the dark castle. Coming in fast and furious, the dragons got closer to the castle, their roars getting louder and louder. When they were low enough they began to shoot fire from their mouths down upon the castle walls. Mindy flew in much lower and flew past the castle wall and into the courtyard, and with one blast of breath, she lit a bale of hay on fire. Melinda followed, a wagon in the middle of the courtyard loaded with supplies was her target, and with a fiery roar, she set the wagon ablaze.

The knights' attempts to shoot arrows at the dragons failed as the dragons were too swift and avoided every shot. Megan watched in horror when ORMR swept down and grabbed one of the stewards. Megan cried out to him, *"No! Please stop, don't harm him!"* ORMR turned his head, saw Megan and dropped the steward before getting too high into the air. The steward landed hard, breaking his ankle. Megan ran over to him, looking up as she cried out to ORMR, *"Why are you doing this?"* She then turned to the King, *"Why are we doing this?"*

ORMR flew once around the castle and then came back down and landed in the middle of the courtyard. The King's knights were watching from the castle wall. They readied their arrows, aiming them at ORMR as he landed near Megan, waiting for the King's command to fire.

Megan could hear ORMR's voice in her head, *"Quick get on my back and we can fly out of here!"* ORMR had come to rescue Megan from the knights. He believed that they had come in the night and taken her from him. But Megan did not climb onto ORMR's back. Instead she replied, *"This is my King and these are his knights,"* she pointed to King James and to the men on the castle walls ready to shoot.

ORMR looked over at King James and then up at the knights on the wall and he replied, *"I thought you were our princess, but it now appears that you are our enemy. You tricked us into believing you would help us nurture our young."* Megan shook her head as she replied, *"We want to live in peace."* Reaching for her bag, she pulled out the book of dragons, *"We were once allies, and we do not want to be afraid of you or for you to fear us. This book tells of the lost legend of how we came to be allies. Can we not be allies again?"* Megan asked.

ORMR looked at King James in the eye. The King was not aware of a lost legend. He only knew of the destruction and fear the dragons once rained down upon his kingdom. King James approached Megan, taking the book from her hand, *"What is this lost legend you speak of?"* He looked at the open page and saw a drawing of a dragon standing side by side with a King. His great grandfather?

ORMR lowered his neck, shook his head and off fell the blue butterfly armor from his back. Megan stepped forward and put the suit of armor on. Once she put on the wings, everyone could hear ORMR speaking to Megan. ORMR spoke knowing that all could hear him now. *"If your King is willing, then we can once again be allies as we once were. I knew your great grandfather. We can live in peace once again if you agree to help us. The full moon is tomorrow. We must complete the incubation period so that Mindy and Melinda's eggs can hatch. Otherwise they will sleep for another hundred years."*

The King was not so sure about the alliance and wanted something in return. He asked, *"The legend also speaks of a boy who will appear from the future. As long as he is present in this time, there can be no peace between us. We need to send him back. This book speaks of a blue butterfly and a potion to return him to his time. This also needs to happen by the full moon."*

ORMR was wise and knew of both legends, the known and the lost. *"Yes I am aware of the boy, the one who looks like your son the prince. We must first get more pollen from the yellow Goldenrod flower on the cliffs. We are in need of one last coating of pollen to complete the incubation of the eggs. You will need the remainder of the pollen to complete the potion to send the boy back to his time."* The King nodded in agreement and their alliance was set.

Megan climbed onto ORMR's neck and off they flew to the mountain cliffs to collect more pollen. Mindy and Melinda who had been flying above the castle turned and flew back to the mountain. They were flying towards the hidden entrance not blocked by the avalanche. Once there, they would wait for ORMR and Megan's return.

When the pollen was collected, ORMR and Megan completed their task by delivering the pollen to Mindy and Melinda. After the last coating of pollen was applied, it was only a short while until the eggs began to hatch. A dozen baby dragons were chipping away at their shells. Once ORMR saw this, he and Megan flew back down to the dark castle. They would only have six hours to fly to the great tree. Megan remembered reading a charm in the book of dragons to speed his flight. Megan and the King climbed onto ORMR's back. She opened the book and read the charm. ORMR flew faster than he ever had before and they arrived at the great tree before midnight.

Lady Elizabeth, Prince Samuel, two knights and Thomas had proceeded to the great tree. The raven never arrived with the final note telling Lady Elizabeth how to send Thomas back. They were unaware of the events that happened at the dark castle. Lady Elizabeth had found another passage in one of her evil spell books. She was desperate and was planning to use this spell if she had to. On top of her walking staff, she mounted her crystal. The book of dark spells was in her black bag with the blue butterfly. They approached the tree. The guards were holding Thomas between them.

Prince Samuel standing nearby observing the ritual was scared and unsure of what was about to happen.

Lady Elizabeth began reading the spell.

Dark as night, moon shining bright
Bring the wind,
Bring the clouds
Bring the thunder, lightning and rain
Send this boy back from whence he came

The wind began to pick up, stronger and stronger and the clouds moved in, covering the light of the moon. Lady Elizabeth pulled the blue butterfly from the net in her bag. The crystal on top of her staff began to shine brightly replacing the light that was blocked out by the clouds. The guards were holding Thomas, and all of them were getting a little frightened. How could it be possible that a storm could be called up like this? Lady Elizabeth released the butterfly and continued to read the spell. She motioned for the guards to force Thomas into the great tree's opening.

Dark as night, moon shining bright
Bring the wind,
Bring the clouds
Bring the rain pouring down
Bring the thunder, hear it roar
Bring the lightning scorch the soil
Send this boy back from whence he came
With Wings of blue, light and rain

Just as she was about to read the final few lines of the spell, the tower bells began to ring. The knights on duty had spotted a dragon approaching. ORMR was making his way down from the clouds. *"Stop!"* he cried, *"Stop!"* All could hear his words since Megan was wearing her wings. Lady Elizabeth and the others turned and looked up.

ORMR landed just ten feet from them.

King James and Megan climbed off of ORMR's back. Megan spoke, *"Lady Elizabeth I have the final ingredient, you will need this to complete the spell."* With that she handed her a vile with the yellow goldenrod pollen.

Samuel ran over to Megan and his father. *"Megan I was so worried about you! Father I did not know what to do, we had to start as it is almost midnight."* Thomas was still standing between the two guards. Samuel turned to him, *"I am sorry, we must send you back. It will be alright, I know it. We have the missing ingredient."*

Megan, Thomas and Samuel hugged each other. The blue butterfly that Lady Elizabeth had caught then landed on Thomas's shoulder. *"I'm ready,"* Thomas said, *"Send me back. I will never forget you all."* Thomas moved to the entrance of the great tree. Lady Elizabeth added the yellow Goldenrod pollen to her potion and read the spell once more.

Dark as night, moon shining bright
Bring the wind,
Bring the clouds
Bring the thunder, lightning rain
Send this boy back from whence he came
Dark as night, moon shining bright
Bring the wind,
Bring the clouds
Bring the rain pouring down
Bring the thunder, hear it roar
Bring the lightning scorch the soil
Send this boy back from whence he came
With Wings of blue from this butterfly
A potion yellow as the sun
Bring a peace for everyone

Just as she finished reading the last line of the spell, lightning struck the top of the great tree.

Thomas instinctively stepped inside the opening at the base of the tree. There was a puff of smoke and he and the blue butterfly were gone.

The wind stopped blowing and the clouds

cleared away. The moon was once again shining down on the great tree and castle. ORMR spoke, *"I need to return to my family, I have twelve little ones to raise now. You will not see us unless you need our help. You can feel safe now."* With that, ORMR flew back to the mountain range. The others walked back to the castle. Tomorrow would be another day.

The sun rose early the next day, not a cloud in the sky, Thomas Senior was already awake, dressed and ready to continue the search for his son. Two days ago the local magistrate had informed him they would have to call off the search. Thomas Senior was not going to give up. He planned to head up to the field today to search once again for any clue that the authorities may have missed. As he approached the great tree at the top of the hill, he noticed a butterfly. He knew his son had an interest in butterflies. He got close enough to see that this was not a common butterfly. This one had blue wings. He watched as it flew into the tree's opening.

Thomas Senior poked his head inside. He stumbled, kicking some stones into the opening. One of the stones hit Thomas Junior on the head as he lay on the ledge below.

Thomas called out, *"Is someone there? Please help me, help me, I'm down here...I'm down here."* Thomas Senior recognized his son's voice at once. He called down, *"It's Dad! I've found you, I've found you!!! Are you alright? I will go and get help and get you out of there."*

Thomas had been missing for two weeks before being found by his father. When the emergency squad arrived, it took several hours to rescue him.

After being taken to the hospital, Thomas laid in his bed and wondered, *"Was it all just a dream?"*

The End